Impacted!
Mickie B. Ashling

Dreamspinner Press

Published by
Dreamspinner Press
4760 Preston Road
Suite 244-149
Frisco, TX 75034
http://www.dreamspinnerpress.com/

Impacted!

Photo by Roberto Chiovitti - www.robertochiovitti.it
Cover Design by Mara McKennen

ISBN: 978-1-61581-023-9

Printed in the United States of America
First Edition
August, 2009

eBook edition available
eBook ISBN: 978-1-61581-024-6

To Jeannie G.,
who continues to be
the most dedicated beta
any writer could ever hope for.
Thank you for keeping up
with my frantic pace
and always watching my back.

and

To the members of my critique group:
Ann, Carolyn, Jackie, Jan, Jeannie,
Laurie, Lyn, Ondina, Patty, and Sharon.
This couldn't have happened without
your consistent feedback and support.

Chapter 1

SCOTT stood at the entrance of the club, waiting for his eyes to adjust to the dim lights, his body tightening with anticipation as music washed over him. Stopping in San Ramon had seemed like a good idea. He'd been browsing the Internet last night, searching for BDSM clubs, and this one had popped up with a three-star rating. He supposed that it was some kind of sign, since he'd have to drive right by it on his way home to San Francisco. He was on the last leg of a monthlong vacation, and right now he was looking for what he needed, hoping to end it with a bang.

So far nothing seemed any different. The music, the lights, and the men were nothing special. The dance floor was packed with hot guys gyrating against each other, shirtless or practically shirtless, in their wife-beaters and cutoffs, showing the bodies that were their only form of currency. The rippling muscles were so much a part of being an attractive gay man that one was almost compelled to appear naked to show off the merchandise.

On the surface, it looked like any other club, but he knew there was another area in the building where people could go to participate in a form of entertainment that was still considered deviant and perverse. This was the final frontier of sexual liberation, the dark side of loving that people hid away, considering it to be shameful and socially unacceptable. To Scott, it was as necessary as breathing.

He stood there in his faded jeans and simple black shirt scanning the room, hoping to see someone out of the ordinary. He didn't plan on settling tonight. He'd already spent the whole month tolerating mediocre hook-ups for the simple reason that nothing better was around. He knew that his expectations were impossibly high and that so far everyone had fallen short. But he was the eternal optimist, the glass-half-full guy who was convinced that the man of his dreams did, in fact, exist. He was looking for the impossible. He wanted romance within a D/s relationship; a love connection with a strong and dominant man.

He tried to picture what someone else would see, watching him standing at the door. He was slightly older than the rest of the men here tonight, carrying his thirty-three years very well. He had high cheekbones, a smooth forehead, and a mop of honey-colored hair that he wore longer than most men in his profession, which only added to the illusion of youth. He ran a hand through it, pushing the strands out of his eyes, a habit that was so much a part of him.

He licked his full lips, making them appear even more enticing. His eyes were his trump card, the *pièce de résistance* that always got him the prize. When he settled them on a man of his choice, he was pretty hard to ignore. They were a clear green, the color of wet leaves after a spring shower, fringed by dark blond eyelashes.

Five minutes at the door convinced him that his side trip seemed like a waste of time. There was no one who attracted him. He decided to have a drink before making the trip back to the city, and he moved over to the bar and waited for someone to take his order. His eyes scanned the dance floor again, hoping he'd missed something, but there was nothing that was remotely interesting.

"What can I get you?"

He turned at the sound of the voice and stared into the blue eyes of the twenty-something-year-old asking the question. Scott was pleasantly surprised at the sight of the man looking at him expectantly. He had a light dusting of freckles on his nose and a mass of unruly curls in a burnished copper color. His teeth shone straight and white, always a plus in Scott's eyes.

"I'll have a Corona with a twist."

"You got it."

The bartender turned and pulled a bottle out and popped the cap, stuck a twist of lime into the opening and handed it to Scott. "Is there anything else I can get you?"

"Are you on the menu?"

He laughed quickly, a blush licking his cheeks. Scott was charmed.

"Not while I'm on the job."

"What's your name?"

"Red."

"What time do you get off?" Scott was intrigued and was hoping to see some sign of interest on the other man's part. He hadn't moved from his spot in front of him, which boded well.

"My shift ends in thirty minutes."

"I can wait, if you want me to?"

Scott saw the relief wash over Red's face. "I'd like that," he said, wiping up the counter and pocketing the change someone had left for him. "Let me know if I can get you anything else."

"Sure thing."

Red grinned and then winked at him before moving off to help another customer.

Scott spent the next thirty minutes alternately watching the dancers and turning back to observe Red. He seemed to have the art of bartending down pat, moving effortlessly from customer to customer. Scott took this opportunity to stare at him shamelessly, his eyes moving up and down Red's body unobserved. He was wearing loose cargo pants and a light blue sleeveless T-shirt that was probably two sizes too small. It stretched across a torso that was well formed, showing off arms that bulged in all the right places. They were well defined but not grotesque, covered with a light layer of reddish fuzz, landscaped with the light brown freckles that usually plagued natural redheads. He tried to imagine what Red looked like without clothes on and was surprised at how quickly his body reacted to the visual.

The man wasn't good looking in the true sense of the word. He was sharp contrasts with his bright red hair and milky white skin, but he had a natural grace and moved like a dancer. He was confident and quietly sexy, making jokes with the customers. The guys seemed to love him, as clearly evidenced by the overflowing tip jar. He was about six feet tall, which suited Scott just fine. He preferred men who were his height. Red's pants fit nicely around a perfectly shaped ass, and Scott's breath caught in his throat and the blood rushed to his groin when he saw the outline of what looked like handcuffs in Red's back pocket. He took another sip of his drink, hoping to still his excitement.

About five minutes to twelve, an older guy walked in and stepped behind the bar. He patted Red on the back and wished him a good night. He must have been the owner, because he seemed very proprietary and everyone knew him. Red looked over at Scott and raised an eyebrow. "Ready?"

"You bet." Scott drained his beer and stood to join him.

In the parking lot, he headed to his car, assuming Red would follow. He felt a hand grab his and pull him roughly against him, crushing him with an open-mouthed kiss that was anything but gentle.

"I've been dying to do this all night," Red moaned, crushing Scott's mouth with an aggressive kiss that left no room for argument. Scott's response was immediate, the groan coming from deep in his chest, inciting Red to pull him closer. They explored each other's mouths, wrestling for control with their tongues. Red won the battle, nibbling and sucking on Scott's lower lip before slipping his tongue into Scott's mouth, tracing the soft inner lip and then pushing against the tentative tongue that sought to explore his. "Your mouth was made for kissing," Red whispered, pulling away for a second to stare into Scott's eyes.

"Kiss me again," Scott urged, pulling Red back to resume the surprisingly delicious foreplay. Kissing a complete stranger wasn't one of Scott's favorite things, but Red was making him forget a few of his own rules. He ran his hands up and down Red's back, resting them lightly on his ass before slipping his hand into Red's back pocket and slowly pulling out the handcuffs.

"I want you to use these on me," Scott said, dangling the cuffs in front of Red's face.

Red grinned. "You like it rough, baby?"

Scott nodded, barely able to croak out the word *yes*.

"Are you going to let me have my way with you?" Red asked seductively, opening up the doors of Scott's vivid imagination.

"Make me scream."

"Where's your car?"

Scott pulled Red toward a dark gray BMW, breaking away from the lip-lock long enough to open the back door. They got into the vehicle and latched onto each other again, exchanging hot kisses while their hands tugged at their clothing.

"Please," Scott begged, watching as Red unzipped his pants and lowered them around his hips, exposing a surprisingly thick cock pulsing with need. Scott bent down and took him in his mouth, moaning his satisfaction while Red grabbed handfuls of Scott's hair and pulled tightly. "God, that feels so good," he said, thrusting slowly against Scott's throat.

Scott worked Red with every technique he knew, taking him deep and caressing him with practiced throat muscles.

"So good, baby...."

"You like that?" Scott asked, ridiculously pleased for some reason. He wanted to make an impression.

"Don't stop."

Scott twirled his tongue around the swollen head, now dotted with drops of moisture that he lapped up, enjoying the sweet, musky taste. He ran his tongue up and down the rigid shaft, nipping at the silky skin, taking a hairless ball into his mouth and rolling it around playfully. He pushed Red and made him lie down on the seat to get better access, yanking off his jeans and tossing them aside. He positioned one of Red's legs on the back of the car seat with the other spread wide to give him more room, and he started licking his perineum, moving his tongue in slow, torturous circles as he listened to the man moaning. He played with the puckered skin around his asshole, flicking his tongue in and out as Red clenched and unclenched, squeezing Scott's tongue with each push. He moved back to concentrate on Red's cock, swallowing him to the hilt, pressing his nose up against Red's pubic bone, working him again with throat muscles that could make a grown man weep.

"I'm close, dude."

Scott nodded, and he felt Red shoot. He swallowed easily, creating even more tension around the pulsating cock, and he reveled in the noises that were coming out of Red's mouth, the sounds of pleasure accompanying each spurt of hot liquid burning its way down his throat. Finally, when the noises stopped, he moved up to Red's face and kissed him, sharing the ejaculate that still coated his tongue.

"Outstanding blowjob." Red huffed, trying to catch a breath.

"My pleasure. Now, tie me up, and do your thing."

Red laughed, delighted by Scott's aggressiveness, and he switched places with him, pulling off the black T-shirt and undoing Scott's belt buckle. His breath caught in his throat when he saw that there was nothing between Scott and his jeans. "Shit, I love a guy that goes commando."

"Fuck me."

"Christ," Red replied, grabbing the waistband and tugging at Scott's jeans. He growled when he saw the erection that bobbed enticingly. "You ready to be my slut boy?"

"Yes."

His hands moved up Scott's torso and rested on his nipples, twisting them sharply, loving the sounds as Scott whimpered in pain.

"Like that, my beautiful pain slut?" Red looked up quickly and saw Scott's eyes were closed. He took the handcuffs and slipped them through the door handles before attaching them to Scott's wrists.

"Tell me what you want, baby."

"Hurt me," Scott begged, thrashing against Red, moaning loudly when he felt the first bite on the soft skin of his inner thigh even as the strong hands twisted nipples that were rock-hard and aching. "Please," he begged again, inciting Red to clench the thighs that were spread wantonly, digging in his nails as Scott rutted against him.

Red sat back on his heels and slapped Scott's ass, cherishing each moan that came out of the beautiful lips, following it up with a series of open-handed slaps on Scott's thighs and balls. He bent down and rubbed his cheek against hot and inflamed skin, every nerve ending alive with sensation.

"Please...."

"What, baby?

"Fuck me," Scott pleaded, pushing Red into rooting around in his pants pocket for the condom that was always on stand-by. He tore at the packet with his teeth, rolled the lubricated sheath onto his distended cock, and pushed into Scott without preamble, into the sweetest vise that gripped him like a soft hand as the blond hissed and thrashed underneath him.

"Jesus, fuck," Red exclaimed, shutting his eyes, swept along by the powerful current of heat that was coursing through his veins as Scott pushed against him, digging his heels into the soft leather of the car seat to get better leverage. He pounded into Scott, thrusting roughly against him, grabbing onto the blond hair and pulling hard, wrenching a gasp out of Scott as he lay trapped underneath him.

"Like that, slut boy?"

"Yes," Scott acknowledged, twisting his lower body and moving against the hips that rolled around expertly, nudging his prostate.

Red bent down and kissed him savagely, biting his lower lip, drawing a few drops of blood, and Scott shuddered through his orgasm, spraying Red's torso and neck with ropes of hot semen that kept on coming and coming and coming as Scott screamed, bucking his hips and thrashing against the body that drilled him without letting up until finally, Red came as well, moaning with pleasure as he rode the tight body underneath him, the orgasm traveling with lightning speed all the way up from his groin to explode out his brain.

"Holy fucking shit," Red groaned, collapsing on Scott, listening as their combined heartbeats knocked against their chests.

Eventually, they had to move. Red pulled off the key that was hanging on a chain around his neck and unlocked the cuffs, rubbing each of Scott's wrists to make sure the blood was circulating properly.

"You okay?" he asked, looking down at the stranger who lay completely sated underneath him.

"More than okay," Scott replied dreamily. "Can I see you again?"

"I'd love to hook up again, baby. You were incredible, so fucking responsive."

"But?"

"I'm leaving town tomorrow."

"Shit!"

"I know," Red answered in a voice deep with regret. "I would have enjoyed getting to know you," he said, pulling on his pants and scrounging for his shirt.

"Are you going far?" Scott asked, picking up his clothes.

"Yeah."

"You think you'll be back?"

"I doubt it."

Scott moved over and kissed Red soundly on the lips. "Story of my life." He laughed ruefully, moved away, and slipped his shirt on.

Chapter 2

SCOTT ripped off his gloves and tossed them into the trash. He'd just finished placing six implants into his patient's lower jaw and was getting ready to dismiss her. Three hours of work that yielded twelve thousand six hundred dollars wasn't bad. He could get used to those numbers.

"Kim will give you all your post-op instructions and my pager number in case you need me later on. You shouldn't have too much discomfort, but if you feel any pain, take the Vicodin. Don't be a martyr, Mrs. Peterson."

"I won't, Dr. Gregory. Thank you so much."

"You're quite welcome. I'd like to see you in a week."

Scott made his way down the hall and into his small office. He glanced at the pink message slip on his desk and was surprised to see the name of the missed caller. He hadn't heard from Susie in at least a year, but he was thrilled she'd called. It would be nice to talk to someone who really knew him.

He picked up his cell phone and keyed in her number.

"Hello?"

"Sue! What a shock!"

"Scotty, hey! Thanks for calling back."

"What's going on, girly? It's been a while."

"I know! I'd heard you moved out there, and I've been meaning to get in touch with you, but somehow things just got away from me."

"Are you still in Chicago?" Scott asked. He and Susie met at Northwestern University where he was taking his prerequisites before enrolling in dental school. She was getting her bachelor's degree in liberal arts. They met in a biology class and hit it off, sharing a passion for blood and guts, much to his delight. Finding a friend who didn't mind the sight of blood or discussing diseases of the mouth was always a challenge, but Susie seemed more than comfortable with all of it. So much so that she'd become a dental assistant.

"How did you end up in San Francisco?" she asked. "Last I heard, you were practicing in Raleigh?"

"I got lucky, Sue. I was offered a partnership in a damn good practice, and I jumped on it. You know how much I've wanted to move out here."

"The land of the rainbow flag."

"Hey, none of that."

"What? Don't tell me you're in the closet again?"

"For a while. The guy who owns this practice isn't exactly a free thinker."

"Scott, why do you do these things to yourself?"

"Listen, I haven't heard from you in over a year, and I don't need a lecture. I had enough of those when I was seeing you on a daily basis."

Susie laughed on her end, the same laugh he remembered so well, and it made him realize how lonely he'd been since his move. Other than the people here at the office, he'd hardly made any friends, choosing to stick close to home after work rather than risk being found out.

"Are you coming out to the Bay Area? I'd love to see you."

"I'm actually thinking of leaving Chicago, and I wondered if you might need an assistant?"

"No way! I'd love it! The girl who's helping me now is a temp and not really that great. It'll be nice working with someone who knows what she's doing."

"Are you serious?"

"Absolutely! When can you start?"

Susie laughed again, that rich laugh that always made him smile, it was so contagious. "Give me a few weeks, will you? I've got shit to do before I can leave."

"Like what?"

"Like get rid of my apartment, quit my job, pack. You know. Stuff."

"Yeah. What about your mom?"

"She's in a nursing home. We had to transfer her about six months ago."

"I'm sorry to hear that."

"She doesn't even know who I am anymore."

"Shit," Scott said quietly, feeling instant empathy for Susie. He knew how devoted she was to her mother.

"Is this why you're moving?"

"I'm so bored, Scott. I feel like my life is going nowhere, not to mention that my love life sucks big time."

"What's the matter? Have they run out of Latinos in the Windy City?"

"Shut up!"

"Well, don't fret. I'm sure there's someone out here who you can devour in your usual style."

"You think so? Are there any straight men in that city?"

"Of course there are; I just don't know any," he said ruefully. He didn't know any gay men either, which wasn't surprising because he'd been living like a monk since he'd moved. He leaned his head on his high-backed chair and allowed himself to think about that guy in San Ramon. His cock twitched when he thought back to their short meeting. He'd give anything to see him again.

"Scott?"

"I'm here, Susie."

"I thought I lost you."

"No, just zoned out for a sec. So, when can I expect you?"

"Give me three weeks."

"Okay. Do you want me to find you a place?"

"That would be great. Make sure they take pets."

"Are you bringing Simon?"

"I would sooner leave my left kidney."

"Christ! You and that cat are attached at the hip."

"He's family, Scott."

"All right, already. So you want an apartment that allows pets. How about a view? Is that important?"

"Only if it's nine inches with a fine set of balls to go with it."

"I see that you and I are going to be fighting over the same men again."

"Most likely, but at least I do something about it!"

"Hey! Is that the way to talk to your prospective boss?"

"Sorry, boss. Tell me you have a partner or at least a boyfriend?"

"Nope."

"Scott!"

"Shh. Behave," Scott admonished, even though he secretly loved her bantering. She was more than just a good friend to him. She knew him inside and out.

"Listen," Susie said, "I'm so excited about this! I can hardly wait to see you."

"I am too, Suz. Get your pretty butt over here as soon as you can. I'll e-mail you the links to the apartments. What's your address?"

"Susiebrioni at Gmail."

"Got it. You should be hearing from me in a few days."

"Thank you, Scott. You have no idea how relieved I am."

"It'll be nice to have you around," he said gently, meaning every word. "Talk to you soon, okay?"

He hung up and looked at his schedule. There was time for a quick sandwich before starting the afternoon, so he threw on a jacket and made his way out of the office. He decided to run over to the basement at Macy's. The food court was surprisingly good, and there was usually a table available so he didn't have to eat standing up.

It took about fifteen minutes before he was actually seated and biting into his turkey and Swiss. The bag of jalapeno-flavored potato chips lay open, tempting him, and he threw one in his mouth and crunched down.

Susie Brioni. How lucky could be get? Having her assist would not only solve the problem of finding competent help, it might even assuage some of the isolation he was feeling since he'd moved out West. He missed having someone to talk to and go out with.

He's been out here for three months now and was just getting comfortable with his surroundings. San Francisco was everything he'd hoped it would be. The city was beautiful; the variety and quality of the food was unbelievable. He'd never really been a foodie, but since moving to California, he'd begun to appreciate fine food and wine. It also kept him away from the clubs and temptation.

He knew he was being paranoid, but his entire future was riding on this contract with Ron. It would be worth it in the end. In the meantime, he would endure his state of celibacy and suffer for a while.

Having Susie around might be a good way to circumvent Ron's curiosity about his nonexistent love life. She'd been a great beard for him in the past, so it would be a natural thing for them to pick up where they'd left off. In any case, other than that hot guy in San Ramon, he hadn't seen anything to tempt him, which was a good thing, he supposed.

SUSIE said her goodbyes to Scott and put her phone away before she unlocked the door to her apartment. She felt the brush against her leg before she heard the purring. Simon was her ten-year-old Himalayan with a personality that reminded her constantly who was boss. He butted his head against her chin and purred like a small power tool as she nuzzled his warm neck; blowing on his face and giggling when he made the little hissing noises that let her know he wasn't amused. She left him on the kitchen table and went over to the pantry to dig out a can of Fancy Feast, and she scooped out half of the tuna in his glass dish and placed it in front of him so that he could eat his late dinner while she had hers.

She chewed on the deep-dish spinach and garlic pizza, barely tasting what would normally be one of her favorite meals. She was mentally exhausted, worn out from a life that seemed to be all about duty and not enough fun. The daily visits to the nursing home to look in on her mother were finally getting to her. It would have been worth it if she was recognized, but the sad lady in the wheelchair was not the woman Susie had grown up with. That vibrant, attractive blonde had disappeared, and the withered shell with the gray hair and the vacant blue eyes was no one she knew. Her visits were more for her own state of mind than her mother's, who had no idea who Susie was. Yet Susie continued to stop by every night on her way home from work to bring her a daisy, her favorite flower. The nurses thought her gesture made a difference; they seemed to think that a spark of life would flare in the old lady's eyes when they replaced the flower in her tiny bud vase, but Susie knew better. No one was home in that brain.

It was becoming more and more obvious that she needed to make a change. She was thirty years old and in her prime, but she had nothing to show for it. No husband or children to keep her in Chicago, no family to speak of other than her invalid mother and a stepfather she wasn't close to. The only time she remembered his existence was when she received his monthly check, a bonus from the trust fund her mother set up years before her mental breakdown. He was one in the long line of men who had littered her formative years, but he'd actually married her mother and stuck around, unlike all the other shadowy figures who had moved in and out of her mother's bedroom, usually leaving early in the morning before the kid would wake up. Or so her mother thought.

She didn't realize that her daughter heard everything at night as she lay in bed, clutching her pillow. Susie could never figure out what the fights were about, but the noises of passion, the drunken weeping, the repeated words of anger and abuse the men would hurl at her mother were a constant thing she had to endure.

It was around that time that Susie began to pleasure herself, discovering the joys of sexual release through masturbation. Nothing else seemed to calm her down or lull her into a state of forgetfulness. She had become so adept at it that when she finally reached the age of puberty and started dating, she found most of the boys to be lacking. They were inexperienced and inept, and when she told them what they needed to do to make her happy, they resented her and found her controlling. It was a pattern that kept repeating, like the hot dogs at a lousy Cubs game.

It seemed as if she'd had better choices a few years ago, but her selection was getting more and more limited. She had exhausted the gene pool at all the neighborhood bars, or maybe she was getting more discriminating with age. Who knew? What she did know was that she was bored and restless.

Marriage wasn't an option for her. She'd sworn it away years ago when she stopped believing in happy endings. Her biological father took off when she was only four, choosing freedom over the love of a little girl and her mother. Susie didn't believe in love and monogamy. Her family was living proof that it was an unattainable goal.

She opted for adventure instead, for a life filled with beautiful men and good sex. Susie craved that magical feeling of first encounters, that gut-wrenching attraction that one could only achieve with someone new. The thrill of finding a guy who'd let her be on top and tie him up once in a while was her constant goal. Elusive, but achieved on rare occasions.

She supposed that many people considered her opinions on sex and marriage to be a bit extreme. Men balked at her aggressiveness, turned off by her need to be in charge. She knew no other way. The few times she'd tried to act the gentle and submissive partner had been a disaster, and the men could tell it was all an act and not really who she was.

Susie believed in hard work tempered with hard play. She was well aware of all her responsibilities and had no problem taking them on, but she felt she'd earned her right to mess around whenever the need arose. She'd gone to college and was in the work force, even though no one could understand her interest in dentistry. She wasn't sure what attracted her about the profession, but she enjoyed every minute of it. She'd been a dental assistant for almost seven years and was damned good at her job.

Calling Scott was a brilliant move on her part. She'd forgotten what a good friend he could be since they'd parted ways, but hearing his voice tonight had reminded her of all the good times they'd had together.

Scott was a brilliant periodontist with hands of gold. She'd never assisted anyone else who was quite as good. He was easy to be around and low-key, not high-strung or egocentric like a lot of surgeons she'd worked with. He was gentle with his patients, yet always on the cutting edge of technique, more than capable of performing whatever was necessary to bring someone back to good periodontal health.

It would be an easy transition for her, now that she knew where she was going and who her employer would be. Even with her trust fund, she needed something to do and money to do it with. She couldn't get very far on two thousand dollars a month. Not the way she liked to live. Having this job would give her freedom of choice, something she was rabid about.

She got up and started stripping on her way to the bathroom, pausing at the full-length mirror to appraise her body ruthlessly. Her breasts were full and well-formed. They were also natural, not store bought. Her stomach was flat, her long legs firm and golden brown, thanks to the biweekly tanning sessions. Her chestnut-colored hair was the only legacy her Italian father left her. It fell in thick waves around her shoulders and had bronze and gold highlights. Her eyes were Romanesque as well, heavy-lidded and framed by perfectly arched eyebrows that looked painted on. Her hazel eyes were expressive and mirrored all her emotions, often times too easily. She had yet to master the talent of hiding her feelings.

After her shower, she grabbed a thick towel and wrapped it around herself, twisting her hair in another one. In the bedroom, she grabbed for her phone, speed dialing her stepfather, eager to be done with this conversation.

"Susie." The voice on the other line was terse, annoyed because she'd woken him. "Do you have any idea what time it is?"

"I'm sorry. I just thought you should know that I'm planning to leave Chicago."

"Where are you going?"

"San Francisco. You need to make alternative arrangements for Mom."

"Your mother will be just fine. She won't even know you're gone."

His words cut to the quick, reinforcing what she already knew. "I realize that, however, it would make me feel a lot better if you would visit her occasionally."

"I try and make time for her, Susie, but I'm a busy man."

"I know."

"Why the sudden urge to move?"

"I'm bored out of my mind."

"Why don't you go on a trip? Boredom is no reason to leave town."

"Nah… I'd just have to come back here. I need to get a life."

"Listen, you do what you have to do. Your mother's arrangement in the nursing home won't change with your departure. She has the best of care."

"I'm aware of that, Dad. I would just feel better if I knew she had some human contact if I were to leave."

"She'll be fine," he said again, shifting tone slightly. Susie could tell he was uncomfortable with the entire conversation and where it was heading.

"Will you visit her once in a while?"

"I'll try."

"Thank you."

"When do you plan to move?"

"As soon as I get rid of my apartment and pack my things,"

"Why don't you let me take care of that? I can have you packed and moved in a few weeks if it's what you really want."

"I do. In fact, I already have a job."

"Well, that's a plus. When did you do that?"

"I just spoke to my friend, Scott Gregory. He's in practice in San Francisco and needs an assistant."

"That's great! Let's talk about this in the morning, Susie. It's late."

"I know, Dad. I'm sorry I woke you." She hung up, relieved that she'd gotten that out of the way. Her stepfather was a stranger in many ways, yet she couldn't fault him for his financial support. His checkbook was always ready when she or her mother needed it. It was a different story when it came to feelings. They had never connected on an emotional level. He was the man her mother had married, and she had resented him from the beginning, shutting him out of her heart completely. Maybe if she'd let him into her world, they'd have been closer, but she'd been convinced he'd walk out, just like all the other men. He'd proven her wrong and had stuck it out, caring for a woman who he loved in his own fashion.

She continued to think of San Francisco as her potential new home. She'd been there several times, but it was years ago, when she was much younger and unable to explore the nightlife. It was a charming city, no doubt about that, with its hills and streetcars and fabulous food. The restaurants stood out in her brain since her stepfather owned so many of them. She recalled visits to North Beach and platters heaped with Dungeness crab.

She threw on a nightgown and turned off the lights before she slipped into bed. For the first time in months she relaxed, knowing her life was about to change direction. She realized that she was borderline depressive and this feeling of ennui was a symptom of her present situation. It would do her a world of good to get away and embark on this new adventure. Knowing she had a friend and a confidant waiting for her in a new city was the only thing that put a smile on her face just before she dozed off.

Chapter 3

ROBIN sat on a stone bench in Union Square, taking sips out of his iced coffee. He was killing time… waiting until seven-thirty to enter the building and take the elevator up to the sixteenth floor. It was his first day of work, and he was anxious to get started.

The last time he'd been here was for his interview, and even though all had gone well and Dr. Morris had seemed very nice, it was his first job in his chosen field, and he was apprehensive. It was one thing to work on patients in hygiene school. It was another thing altogether to have a paying customer, someone who would be judging him from the minute they sat in his chair. Furthermore, a male hygienist wasn't very common, even if this was California and more importantly, San Francisco. Women outnumbered them in the field, fifty to one, and most patients looked at a male hygienist as a dental school dropout.

Robin knew this wasn't the case. He chose hygiene because he loved dentistry, but wasn't willing to spend six years and over one hundred and fifty thousand dollars to become one. He could have gotten a student loan, but didn't want to put himself into hock for the rest of his life. He also had a mother who worked double shifts as a nurse trying to make ends meet, and he refused to burden her with any of his financial needs. His part-time bartending job had supported him and paid for the two-year hygiene program at Diablo Valley College.

He did great in school, always in the top tenth percentile of his class, enjoying the interaction between himself, his teachers, and his fellow classmates, even though ninety percent of them were female. He was meticulous and thorough, borderline anal about certain things. He liked to pick and poke, enjoying himself immensely when a new case would present itself with years of accumulated plaque that he could chisel away at. He derived great satisfaction from a job well done, and when patients thanked him for doing something he found very enjoyable, he was pleased that he'd gone ahead with this career, despite the odds.

Robin took another sip of his coffee, wishing he had a donut or a muffin to go with it. He'd already spent way too much money on his move, and the first and last months' rent had just about broken him. He was down to his last two hundred dollars, and he knew it would be another two weeks before he saw any money, so he was watching every cent.

He'd been self-supporting for years, so he was well aware of how incredibly lucky he was to have found this job. Working at 450 Sutter for a periodontist who'd been in practice for thirty years was a huge break, considering he was fresh out of school and a male to boot. Dr. Morris had been pleasant, but had acknowledged that he'd never had a male hygienist before. He was a little concerned that his associate was on vacation and unable to sit in on the interview, but he went ahead and hired Robin with the understanding that he was on a three-month probation.

He would have never considered him for the job if Robin had told him he was gay. Robin could smell a breeder and a homophobe from miles away, and Dr. Morris was all of those things and then some. Robin recalled the plaques from Promise Keepers that were hanging on the walls beside the diploma from the University of California.

Promise Keepers, the right-wing conservative Christian organization of men who professed to walk in Christ's shoes, dedicated to building strong marriages and families through love, protection, and biblical values. Members were committed to practicing spiritual, moral, ethical, and sexual purity. Dr. Morris would have puked all over his desk and tossed Robin out on his twisted ass if he found out that he was not only gay, but steeped in the world of BDSM.

Robin shook his head and wondered if he were a little crazy for taking this job. He knew he wanted to live in San Francisco. It was a dream he'd had since he was a kid growing up in the East Bay, listening to the jeers and taunts of other boys who made fun of him and called him a homo. He wasn't just a homo, he acknowledged realistically, he was a deviant as well. He knew he was a little kinky in his sexual preferences when he got off on watching DVDs of men in leather brandishing whips and floggers. Eventually, he realized that he was hard-wired that way, just as he was born gay. It wasn't something he'd learned or grown into. It just *was*.

The thought of someone submitting to whatever pain he dished out was a huge turn-on for him. To find a submissive who was willing to take it all for that one glorious moment when the pain shifted into the most sublime ecstasy was the most erotic thing in the world, and he'd made it his quest to learn as much about this brand of love as possible. He was a good Dom, albeit a young one, only having been in the scene for a few years. He much preferred private sessions because he couldn't afford the exclusive clubs with the requisite membership fees and the leather outfits that cost an arm and a leg. He liked having sex with his partners, but didn't really enjoy performing in public. Just another kink to add to the many he already possessed.

Fortunately, he had an unusually understanding mother. She'd raised him by herself, often joking that she was a victim of a drive-by fucking, abandoned by the jerk who impregnated her. She insisted on having the baby though, determined to give him the kind of life she'd never had.

Poor would have been a step up from the depths of society that Denise Kennedy had come from. She was raised on the streets and only survived through the auspices of the Salvation Army and the many shelters it provided. Someone had taken hold of her and realized there was an intelligent, caring person underneath the layers of street smarts and filth, and they'd managed to clean her up and educate her. She struggled for years, but eventually came away with a nursing degree. When she found herself pregnant, she promised to give her child all the love and support she never had. She accepted his sexuality as soon as she realized he was gay.

Robin had never confessed his dark side to her. He was reluctant to talk about his need to dominate and subdue, but the box of goodies he kept in the closet was a clear indication of his sexual preferences. Denise had complete access to all his personal items, but had never mentioned his collection of whips and floggers.

He glanced at his watch and realized he had ten minutes to get up to the office. He threw the empty cup into the trash can and hiked over a couple of streets, crossing through Union Square and then Post Street to finally arrive in front of the ancient building on Sutter Street, famous for housing all of the city's more well-renowned doctors and dentists. Only the best and the brightest paid rent at 450 Sutter.

Robin observed the older gentleman in uniform, greeting and helping people into the elevators, directing them to the different floors and offices they were looking for. He held an elevator for Robin and pressed number sixteen as soon as they stepped into the mirrored box. When he got to his floor, he turned right and stopped in front of a door that had two names on it.

He entered the quiet office and made his way to the staff room. He placed his backpack on the floor in the closet and took off his jacket, revealing the brand new navy blue scrubs that brought out the color of his eyes, a good backdrop for the shiny, copper curls that framed his pleasant face. He walked into Dr. Morris's office for the morning huddle and almost turned to stone when he saw his slut boy holding a cup of coffee, standing in a white gown with the name Scott Gregory embroidered on his left pocket.

Robin stared open-mouthed. Here was the living embodiment of the man he'd been fantasizing about for days. The image of the blond handcuffed to his car door and begging to be fucked leaped into his brain, causing all kinds of mischief in his nether regions. He envisioned Scott's cock, thick and heavy between his legs. Felt the soft flesh underneath his hands as he slapped him, heard the moaning vividly in his head; it was enough to make the blood rush to his cheeks and other parts of his body.

Both men were in shock!

"Scott," Dr. Morris said in his booming voice, "This is Robin Kennedy, the hygienist I was telling you about."

"Pleased to meet you," Scott spoke in a daze, reaching out to take the proffered hand.

"Likewise," Robin replied, squeezing Scott's hand a little too tightly.

"Robin," Dr. Morris continued, "Dr. Gregory will go over our office policies and expectations, right, Scott?"

"Right," Scott answered automatically. "Shall we?" he asked Robin, pointing to his private office.

"You bet," Robin replied, following him out the door.

Scott entered a small room with a desk and a filing cabinet, and he waited for Robin to walk through the door and stand before his desk, looking down at him with a bemused look on his face.

"Close the door, please."

Robin pushed the door shut and said, "Dude, I had no idea!" He waited for Scott's reaction, convinced he'd be fired on the spot.

"Hey, relax will you? I'm trying to process this as well. Have a seat."

Robin sat on the edge of the seat, waiting for the ax to drop. He stared at his employer, who looked beautiful in his doctor's gown, almost as gorgeous as he looked naked and begging. Robin rubbed his face and a small groan escaped his lips.

Scott started to chuckle, the laughter bubbling out of him as he thought about their situation. Robin looked surprised, but he started to smile as well, finally giving in to the hilarity of it all, and the sounds of their voices reverberated in the small office. They laughed so hard tears rolled down their cheeks. "What are the fucking odds that this would happen?" Scott paused in the middle of it all, trying to get it together.

"It's pretty unbelievable, isn't it?" Robin replied, wiping his eyes with the back of his hands.

"I thought your name was Red?"

"It's my nickname. Does Morris even know that you're gay?"

"Hell, no!"

"And a pain slut." Robin grinned.

"Shut up!"

"Why are you in this practice?"

"It's a long story… one I'd rather get into over dinner. You want to meet tonight?"

"Ya think? Do you have any idea how many times I've jerked off with a vision of you handcuffed and begging?"

"God," Scott moaned, running his hand through his hair. "Stop it, or I'll disgrace myself and, we'll both get fired."

"Sorry," Robin replied. "Or not."

"Not?"

"The thought of you shooting all over me will sustain me all day."

"Will you fucking quit it? Get to work!"

Robin stood and looked down at Scott. "Yes, sir." He smiled. "You realize that you're going to pay for making me call you *sir*."

"Jesus."

Robin bent down quickly and reached across the desk, pulling Scott out of his seat and attacking his mouth with a mind-blowing kiss that left them both breathless. "Have a nice day, Dr. Gregory."

"Get the hell out of here," Scott replied with a stunned look on his face.

Chapter 4

SCOTT had just dismissed his last patient for the day, and he hurried down the hallway, eager to strip off his scrubs and dress in his street clothes. He and Red were going out to dinner. He paused, telling himself that he had better get used to calling him Robin. He was still trying to wrap his head around this bizarre set of circumstances. What were the chances that they'd hook up again, and right here in his workplace? It was going to be a true challenge, melding their private and professional lives. He wasn't quite sure how to proceed.

Scott had looked over Robin's résumé after their morning meeting. He learned that Robin was six years younger than him and that he was from San Ramon. His education seemed first-rate, and there were letters of recommendation from the professors he'd trained under. Everything was clearly laid out on paper.

Of course, nowhere did it mention the fact that Robin was a Dom; part of a secret society the world still considered perverted and deviant. Gay awareness and acceptance had made great strides in Scott's lifetime, yet there was still a huge stigma associated with BDSM. Even the most evolved shied away from admitting to being any part of it. It was no wonder then that most men and women who were into this form of erotica didn't advertise.

Scott discovered his penchant for sado/masochistic love as a late teen. He had hooked up with a guy who was into the rougher side of sex, and it made him realize that there was a side of him that needed the pain as much as it needed the loving. It was something in his makeup that made him crave that one moment when everything shifted into pleasure of the highest intensity.

He made it a point to study this need methodically, the way he did everything else. It was a huge revelation, especially when he went online to look at actual footage of scenes. As soon as he turned twenty-one, he'd gone to a club and become a regular, experimenting with different Doms, seeking to learn more about his likes and dislikes. Eventually, he realized that public scenes weren't his thing. He was far too private and introspective to enjoy anything like that.

He'd never made a romantic connection with any of the Doms he'd been with, and it all felt so cold and scripted. Scott couldn't find the dignity in submitting to someone without the romance. Most people disagreed with him, telling him it wasn't a necessary ingredient; however, he was a romantic at heart. As a result, he never found that one moment of true submission when he gave himself over entirely, putting his life in another's hands and crossing that line between pain and pleasure, the "subspace" everyone seemed to be reaching for.

His chance meeting with the attractive bartender had been somewhat of a revelation in that he'd felt a connection from the very beginning. It was tentative because they'd only had a few hours, but there was something about Red that struck a nerve. It was the first time Scott had asked to see someone again. The first time he'd wanted to stay for seconds and even thirds.

Scott hoped that Red had felt it too, and that it was the reason they were going to have dinner. To get acquainted with each other in public before they moved off to some private place where they could explore the other side of their relationship.

They met downstairs at the entrance of the building rather than leaving the office together. There was just something unspoken that acknowledged it would be the best way. They walked down the street several blocks until they got to Grant Street and then turned left and entered the portals of Chinatown. After maneuvering several streets, Scott led Robin into what looked like some hole in the wall, assuring him that the restaurant had some of the best Szechuan food around.

"You like spicy?" Scott asked as they sat across from each other. The restaurant was so tiny that their knees were practically touching under the table.

"I like hot food."

"Good! There's a dish called Yu Shan shrimp that will make your toes curl."

"My toes usually curl when a sub starts to beg."

"Fuck, Red, can't we wait until we've had our meal?"

"What's the matter? Can't talk about sex on an empty stomach?"

Scott picked up the bottle of beer the waiter had just brought him, and he took a deep gulp of the cold liquid. "You want to start negotiating already? How do you know I'm even interested?"

Robin reached under the table and smiled when he felt the hardness between Scott's legs. "I can smell your need, Dr. Gregory." He ran his tongue around his lips slowly, never taking his hand off Scott's erection, feeling the organ grow under his expert touch. "Tell me what you want, my gorgeous slut."

Scott looked down and let out a shaky groan. "I want...."

"What, baby?" Robin asked gently. "Tell me how I can make it all better."

"Hurt me," Scott whispered, almost afraid to say the words. "Dominate me."

"I would love to," Robin answered. "But first, we need to talk." He shifted in his chair and moved back, removing his hand from Scott's crotch. "Tell me what your limits are."

Scott ran his right hand through his hair, taking a deep breath as he did so, trying to find his center, which seemed to have toppled for a second. "I don't like to be bound."

"You didn't seem to have a problem with the cuffs."

"No, I like that. It's the heavy stuff I don't like. Cages, straight jackets, ball gags. I'm extremely claustrophobic."

"Don't like it or can't handle it? There's a difference."

"I guess I've never been with anyone who made me feel safe enough to handle any of that."

Robin nodded and said, "What about pain? Do you have limits there?"

"Not really, except you can't mark my arms. I wear short sleeves at work."

Robin looked at Scott, noticing how he was fidgeting with the utensils, moving them around as he talked. He reached out and laid a hand on Scott, stilling him for a moment. "It's okay to talk about this, baby. Don't be embarrassed."

Scott laughed a little too quickly. "I'm really nervous for some reason."

"Don't be. I want this to be good for both of us," Robin said, radiating confidence. "Do you have a favorite tool?"

"I like most of them, but I prefer the cane."

Robin whistled. "You really *are* a little pain slut, aren't you?"

"Yes."

"Shall we pick a safe word?"

"Already?" Scott asked, surprised.

"I want you something fierce," Robin stated matter-of-factly. "I've had a raging hard-on since I walked into the office this morning and saw your beautiful face."

"God…."

"Don't you want me?"

"More than anything."

"Good," Robin replied in a low voice. "I just want to be sure we're on the same page."

"Oh, yeah, same page… same book," Scott acknowledged.

Robin squeezed Scott's hand, turning it over and slowly rubbing his thumb in gentle circles on Scott's wrist, moving his fingers up his inner arm. Robin was gratified to see the goose bumps and the light layer of blond hair rising automatically in response to his stroking. The soft march of his fingers turned rougher and he dug his nails into the tender skin near Scott's armpit and saw the instant reaction, even as he heard the first groan. "Oh, my beautiful pain slut," Robin whispered harshly, his arousal clearly evident in his voice. "You're so fucking responsive."

"Red...."

"What, baby?"

"I'm so hard."

"I know... let's pick that safe word."

"It was red, but obviously I'm changing it. How about blue?"

"Whatever works for you, baby."

"Please don't call me that."

"Why not?"

"I don't like it."

"I'll call you whatever I want," Robin answered quietly. His eyes turned steely, never wavering for one second, and Scott felt the thrill of being with a true Dominant for the first time in years. His blood zinged through his veins, almost boiling over with excitement.

"Robin—"

"You can only use my name while we're at work. As soon as we walk out of the building, or even when we're on the phone, you'll address me as Sir. If this evolves into something more permanent, you will call me Master."

"Yes, Sir."

"I have serious misgivings about this," Robin stated, reluctantly pulling his hand away from Scott. "I'm not sure it's wise to mix business with pleasure."

"I hear you, but I think the benefits might outweigh the risks."

"Do you?" Robin asked, secretly thrilled by Scott's response. However, there was no escaping the fact that things would be difficult if they chose to go through with this. He let out a heavy sigh and said, "This is a fucked-up situation, and I honestly don't know if it's going to work. I need this job, Scott, and I don't want to see it jeopardized."

"And you think I don't? My entire future is wrapped up in this contract with Ron Morris."

"How the hell did you end up with him? He's not exactly gay-friendly."

"It was a question of the best deal for me, and he had it."

"Are you planning on staying in the closet forever?"

"Right now, I'm an associate on salary. Ron can change his mind during these first twelve months. It's all part of the agreement."

"And you're positive that no one around here knows the real Scott Gregory?"

"I'm new in town, Robin, just like you. I've kept a low profile since I moved and intend to remain on the down low until this is all a done deal. Then I can come out."

"Where are you from?"

"I'm originally from Michigan. I did my prereqs at Northwestern in Chicago, and then I moved to Boston for my degree. I haven't lived in Ann Arbor for years."

"Were you into the scene in any of the cities you mentioned?"

"Boston."

"Clubs or private?"

"I'm not big on clubs."

"That makes two of us."

"How long have you been a Dom?"

"Officially over two years. Unofficially since I was eighteen."

"What do you mean 'officially'? You need a permit to be a Dom?" Scott asked, a smile tugging at his lip.

"I paid the money and got trained by some of the best."

"There's a school for this?"

"Yes."

"Well, that's a relief. Glad to know that you're well educated," Scott teased.

"It was very intense. I had to experience every tool that was available."

"I see. So are you a switch?"

"No, but a good Dom needs to know how everything feels so he can empathize with his sub."

"Have you ever had a long-term sub?"

"No. Have you ever been in a relationship with one Master?"

Scott shook his head.

"Why don't we just play this by ear?" Robin asked, just before taking a bite out of the steaming hot egg roll the waiter placed on their table. "Let's see how it goes after our first session, and then we can negotiate."

"Okay," Scott replied. Now that business was out of the way, he had a chance to observe Robin up close. He really wasn't what Scott considered to be his type. He'd always fallen for guys with dark hair and beefier torsos. Robin was built like a runner. He was lean and muscular, without an ounce of fat anywhere. His hands and arms were incredibly powerful even without the bodybuilder-bulge. Scott could attest to that, recalling the way Robin held him down so easily that night in the parking lot.

Robin's entire palette was fire and ice, his hair color a burning flame shot through with varying shades of silver and gold that seemed to catch every bit of light in the room. Scott couldn't decide whether he liked it or hated it, but it certainly grabbed his attention. The most outstanding feature on the youthful, freckled face in front of him were the eyes. They were a deep blue, like the hydrangeas that littered the hills of his childhood home, but what made them so unusual was that they could be warm and inviting one minute and then turn cold and cruel as Robin's need to dominate surfaced.

He was looking at him right now, frying Scott with the intensity, almost as if he could read his mind.

"Have you gotten your fill yet?" Robin asked in the Dom voice Scott was starting to recognize. It was the self-assured tone that sent an instant signal to his cock, convincing it to stand and salute. "This will be the last time you look into my eyes this evening."

Chapter 5

SCOTT'S apartment building was on Jackson Street in the Nob Hill area. It was an older edifice with thick walls and creaky elevators decorated in gold leaf and mirrors.

He lived in a two-bedroom unit with an outside view from his living room that explained why his rent was so atrocious. Robin was impressed by the understated elegance and warmth of his surroundings. There were two sofas and an armchair, covered in soft cocoa brown leather that offset the deep red and gold of the oriental carpet. Several paintings lined one wall, and an entertainment center with state-of-the-art video and audio equipment lined the other. The third wall was made of glass with a sliding door that led out to the balcony that afforded a bird's-eye view of San Francisco and the surrounding area.

Robin put his black bag on the hardwood floor next to the front entrance. They'd stopped at his apartment on their way, and Scott had sat in his car while Robin ran up to get his "tool" kit. Neither man spoke on the ride over. It was almost as if they were afraid to say the wrong thing or they were both so engrossed in their feelings and what was about to happen that they didn't want to spoil anything with small talk.

Scott moved over to the entertainment center and turned on the music, selecting a soft jazz to help soothe his jumpy nerves. "Do you want something to drink?" he asked, turning toward Robin, waiting for some direction.

"Come here."

Scott returned to stand in front of Robin with his eyes lowered to the ground.

"Good boy," Robin said gently, pleased with this show of respect. "I want you to take off all your clothes."

Scott started with his shirt, unbuttoning it slowly but picking up speed as his excitement grew. Robin could see his fingers trembling slightly as he fumbled with the cloth, but finally Scott got the shirt off and let it drop to the floor. He paused, giving Robin a few minutes to enjoy the sight of his golden brown body with the requisite six-pack and puffed-out pecs. Robin's first thought was that Scott must do some serious gym time to achieve those results. He said nothing but gazed at the beauty in front of him and was enamored.

Scott continued to undress, unzipping his pants and then pushing them down over his hips, listening to Robin's sharp intake of breath when he saw that Scott was going commando again. Scott didn't dare raise his eyes, but he could tell by the sound of Robin's voice that he was excited.

"Is this for me, or do you hate underwear?"

"Hate it, Sir. It's too confining."

"Interesting," Robin replied in a voice that came out harsh and strangled. "Please proceed."

Scott toed off his shoes and kicked his pants off, watching them flop down beside his shirt. He bent down and pulled off his socks and then stood up and put himself in the display position with his arms behind his back, his hands clasped together and his eyes looking down at the ground. Robin thrilled to the sight of a very respectable cock heavy and swollen between his legs. Scott's pubic hair was light brown and neatly trimmed. His balls were large and shaved, which made the saliva pool in Robin's mouth as he imagined licking them.

"You are perfect."

"Thank you, Sir. I'm glad that I please you."

"You more than please me, baby. I want a taste."

"Sir?" Scott's reaction was evident from the steady rise of his cock as it lengthened and pulled away from his body.

Robin moved toward Scott and lifted his face with both hands. He bent forward and kissed him, pleased that Scott opened his mouth readily, accepting Robin's tongue, allowing it to sweep around his inner lip possessively. Scott met his tongue with a gentle push of his own, waiting to see if this was allowed. When Robin moaned, Scott became more aggressive, pushing his tongue in further, meeting Robin's head-on as they danced around each other in a passionate mix of fluids.

Robin tore his mouth away from lips that were systematically destroying his composure and he transferred his attention to Scott's neck and ears, nipping at the skin with his teeth while Scott writhed and pushed closer.

"You mustn't come, baby, or you'll be punished."

"Please?"

"No!"

Robin stepped back and watched as Scott took a deep breath and tried to will his orgasm away. He seemed to settle down quickly, pleasing Robin with his obvious self-control. Robin bent down and unzipped his bag, pulling out a pair of nipple clamps he had a certain fondness for. They were attached to a silver cock ring by a long chain. He flicked his tongue over Scott's pink buds, watching them harden immediately, and he positioned one of the clamps, loving the sound of Scott's voice as he hissed out in pain. He did the same thing to the other one, clamping it before moving up to Scott's mouth again with a deep kiss that tore a groan out of both of them. "You're doing so good, baby."

"Thank you, Sir."

Robin held the silver cock ring in his hand and said, "I'm putting this on you so you don't come. If you try and take it off, or if your cock gets too distended, it will tighten the chain and pull at your nipples. I suggest you behave, or you'll pay the price."

"Yes, Sir. Thank you, Sir."

"Pleasure me," Robin commanded after he'd placed the cock ring. He pushed Scott down on his knees in front of him. He watched Scott struggling with his zipper, so he reached down to help, pulling his cock free from his briefs, smiling when he saw the look on Scott's face. A starving man gazing on a banquet....

"Take all of it, baby. Show me what you can do," Robin ordered in a voice gruff with desire. Even though he'd received a blowjob that night in the parking lot where they first met, it was hurried. He remembered that it was good, but he was curious to see how much Scott could really do. There was a big difference between what he'd received then and what he was expecting now.

Scott moaned and closed his eyes, wrapping his lips around Robin's cock. His mouth stretched over the thick girth, and Robin watched as the blond sucked him into the wet heat, relishing the moans that came out of his throat as he allowed Robin's cock to slide in so easily. Robin let Scott control the movements to make sure that he wasn't gagging or choking, and when he felt that his sub was comfortable with his size, he pushed himself in further, heartened when he saw Scott could take him all the way down his throat. Robin felt something shatter inside of him at the sight of the beautiful blond on his knees. What he was receiving—this trust that Scott was handing over so graciously—wasn't an everyday occurrence. It took months to build up this level of faith in each other, yet it was being gifted to him by a man who was becoming more and more special in Robin's eyes.

"You're doing beautifully," Robin whispered, his voice cracking a little. He withdrew his cock, pulling away slowly and listening as Scott inhaled deeply, only to follow it up with another push as he swallowed him down again. Scott seemed relaxed, letting his throat muscles caress Robin's cock as it lay deep down his throat. He held him without breathing, knowing one misstep would cause him to strangle, yet Scott seemed to trust that Robin knew what he was doing and he knelt in perfect stillness as Robin slowly withdrew again. He waited to hear Scott take a breath and then pushed back into his mouth, moaning "Yes" with each thrust, lost in the sensation that enveloped him. These steps were repeated several more times until finally, Robin could take no more, and he grabbed Scott's head. "I'm coming," he huffed out as he swayed his hips back and forth, releasing a guttural cry as he exploded into Scott's mouth, staggering with the force of the orgasm as his come pulsated in staccato beats.

Robin pulled Scott up and wrapped his arms around him, waiting to get a better handle on the feelings that had gripped him unexpectedly. He'd come in many a mouth in his lifetime, but this was in a category all on its own. Being the recipient of a trust so freely given by a virtual stranger was the most powerful sign of submission Scott could have offered him.

Robin pushed himself away and said in a barely audible voice. "You've pleased me, baby. I'm going to let you come."

"Thank you, Sir."

Robin held Scott's hand and moved him over to the sofa. "Lie down, facing up." He'd regained some control over his shaky emotions, and this was reflected in his strong and forceful voice as he directed his sub.

Robin took his shirt off and then pushed his jeans and briefs down his slim flanks, standing in front of Scott, who was devouring him with his eyes. "Do you find me attractive?"

"Yes," Scott said, practically holding his breath. "I've never been with a true redhead."

Robin laughed. "You like the red bush?"

"It's very sexy, Sir."

"Hands above your head and don't move! If you do, I won't let you come."

"Yes, Sir."

The nipple clamps and the cock ring looked beautiful against the backdrop of Scott's golden tan. The chain lay flat against his stomach, pulled by the rapidly increasing erection that Scott was trying to control. Robin snapped a flogger against his leg and saw that the sound of the leather against his skin made Scott even harder, and the groan coming out of him was even further proof that he was starting to lose it. Robin held the soft, suede flogger with knots tied at the ends. He knew this tool would only serve as an appetizer for someone who craved a good caning, but it would give him an idea of Scott's threshold, and he wanted to see some pretty stripes on him.

Robin laid the first stroke with a flick of his wrist, watching the pink stripe appear on Scott's thigh, changing to a deep red almost instantly. He raised his hand again and marked Scott's thigh once more, following it up with several steady strokes. He watched as Scott closed his eyes and started to moan, a deep rumbling coming from somewhere inside, giving Robin goose bumps and resurrecting his cock immediately.

"Bend your legs and spread them," Robin ordered, bringing the flogger down in a quick snap so that the tips kissed Scott's balls, eliciting a yelp.

"Hurt, baby?"

"No, Sir… feels good."

Robin smiled, enjoying the sight of Scott naked and wanton in front of him. His erection was pulsing and tumescent, dripping moisture from the shiny pink head that caused the nipple clamps to pull mercilessly. "You are my beautiful slut, aren't you?" Robin said, his voice caressing Scott with its silky tone.

"Yes, yes… your slut, only yours, Sir."

Robin wanted to continue to flog him, but a part of him needed to see Scott's face in the throes of an orgasm, so he put the tool aside and got on his knees in front of Scott and reached for the cock ring to release it. "You've earned this, my sweet one," he said, in a voice husky with desire. "I want to watch you come." He removed the nipple clamps and pressed his mouth to each one, listening to the sound of Scott's soft sighs as he soothed the sting with his tongue. He dug into his bag and pulled out a condom and some lube.

He knelt in front of Scott and rolled the condom on his erection, followed by a generous amount of lube that he also spread on Scott's hole. "You ready?"

"Please."

Robin kissed him quickly and then positioned himself in between the spread legs. He looked down at Scott, who waited expectantly, and he moved, shoving through the tight ring of muscle forcefully. He heard the puff of breath escaping Scott's lungs as he grunted through the first thrust.

"Sir," Scott cried out, lifting his hips off the sofa.

"Jesus...."

"Fuck me! Oh God, Master, Sir, please... don't stop!" Scott babbled, frantically moving his hips against Robin. Robin rode him for a while, thrusting in and out, loving the sounds streaming out of Scott, the hands that clenched his arms, the legs that wrapped around his hips but most of all the face that seemed to light up like a thousand-watt bulb. "Come for me, baby," Robin growled as he reached down and wrapped his fingers around Scott's erection, tugging a few times until he felt the hot liquid pouring over his hand, accompanied by the sweetest sounds coming out of Scott's throat, pulling his own orgasm out of him much too soon. He collapsed on Scott's chest, listening to their combined heartbeats as they came down from that incredible high.

"You were perfection," he sighed into Scott's ear. "You've made me very happy."

"Thank you, Sir."

"Call me Master," Robin said, pushing up on his forearms and staring into the green eyes that were moist with tears.

"Master," Scott said, cupping Robin's face with a gentle hand. "Thank you."

Chapter 6

"FOUR-SIX-FOUR," Ron Morris called out as Jenna recorded the numbers in the patient's periodontal chart. It was a routine exam, something he'd done a million times, easily able to do it while his mind was on something else entirely. He was thinking of his office and all the new people he employed.

Susie had arrived in San Francisco a couple of weeks ago and walked into a job that was prearranged before she even left Chicago. Scott had hired her over the phone and informed him after the fact. Apparently they'd known each other for years.

His decision to bring Scott into the practice was the smartest thing he'd done in a long time. Scott was an exceptional surgeon. He was doing procedures Ron had shied away from because he felt he was too old to be learning new techniques. He didn't dare risk any lawsuits now that he was so close to the finish line. So he passed the more difficult cases to Scott: the sinus lifts and the implants all the baby boomers were begging for. No one wanted to deal with partials or dentures anymore, not with the advent of all the new technology. It was also a virtual gold mine, he soon discovered, as his income increased dramatically after Scott came into the practice.

Ron Morris had been around the periodontal world for almost thirty years and made a name for himself long ago. His list of patients included many of the rich and famous in the Bay Area. He was charming in a Jimmy Stewart sort of way, completely oblivious to the changes in the world around him.

He'd been married twice. His first wife was the mother of his two grown children. His second wife was fifteen years younger than him. She was his trophy wife, a young and eager pharmaceutical rep who wandered into the practice ten years ago, disrupting his afternoon schedule and eventually breaking up his fourteen-year marriage. She'd had him wrapped around her little finger from day one.

Although he practiced in San Francisco and had lived out in the Sunset District for the last forty years, he was unaware—or rather, unwilling—to acknowledge the changes that had occurred in his city, namely the huge influx of gay men. He believed they were freaks of nature, an abomination littering the streets of an otherwise beautiful town. He was one of those people who truly believed that AIDS was God's way of dealing with this problem. His beliefs were fanned by the rhetoric of the bible-thumping organization, Promise Keepers, which he strived to incorporate into his daily life. His guilt over his affair and breakup of his marriage made him even more rabid about trying to be a good Christian to set a fine example.

He was in the winter of his career, more interested in fly-fishing and duck hunting than practicing dentistry. He stuck around to get Scott comfortable and well in tune with the patients he'd been treating for years. He'd hired Scott as an associate after many months of searching for the right candidate, with the plan that he would buy into the practice after a year and eventually become sole owner. It was all worked out by accountants and lawyers, and it was the only thing keeping Ron sane and working each day. It was to his financial advantage to ensure that Scott succeeded, so that he could buy him out. He was *so* done with this practice and more than ready to pass on the baton, or in his case, the handpiece.

He finished up his exam and left the patient in Jenna's capable hands so she could help make her an appointment and answer any last-minute questions. Jenna had been with him for as long as he had been in practice. He remembered hiring her when she was a senior in high school. She was in her fifties now, but had the mind and body of a much younger woman, which was fortunate for him, as she had become an extension of his rapidly uninterested brain. It wasn't unusual for Jenna to direct him during a surgery when his mind wandered off.

He went into his office and sat at his desk. The payroll sheet was in front of him. So many new people! Robin seemed to be working out despite his initial misgivings. The patients didn't seem to care that he was male. He was pleasant enough, always on time and knowledgeable in his field; a nice young man who would go far, in Ron's opinion. With the right woman's influence, he'd have a long and happy life. It was funny that neither Robin nor Scott were married yet. When he was their age, he already had two kids.

He seemed to be surrounded by single people at the moment, and now, with the addition of Susie, he was outnumbered. Susie was a beautiful girl from a very wealthy Chicago family. Ron had no idea why she wanted to be a working girl when she could be flitting away her days on shopping sprees and trips around the world.

Susie was very much an enigma. One could tell she had everything that money could buy and her values were a little skewed when it came to priorities in her spending. She thought nothing of dropping five hundred on a Mark Jacobs purse, yet she could sit as still as a mouse for a three-hour procedure, elbow-deep in blood and spit, and then clean up the mess afterward. He didn't get the whole rationale behind it or what made her tick. He was just glad that she was there.

Maybe he could work on a match between her and Scott. They looked good together, and they obviously had some history, having gone to college in the same city. There was no harm in being married to your assistant. It was a huge advantage in many ways.

He picked up the phone and asked the receptionist if Dr. Gregory was busy. She told him that he seemed to be free at the moment, so he asked her to send him in.

"Hey, did you need anything?" Scott asked, poking his head into the office.

"Scott! Come in and have a seat."

After Scott sat in the leather chair and crossed his legs, Ron asked, "What do you think of Susie?"

"I think she's great!"

"Do you find her attractive?"

"Why?"

"I think she'd be good for you."

"She is good, Ron. I've never had an assistant this good."

"I meant as a girlfriend."

Scott looked at Ron in shock. "Ron, Susie and I are just friends."

"You should take her out after work. Show her the town."

"Where is this coming from, Ron?"

"It's time you settled down, Scott. You're going to be taking over this practice soon and establishing a life in this city. You need a wife and a family."

"I'm sure that when the right person comes along, I'll be able to make that decision."

"Sometimes you need to use your head instead of your heart, Scott. Susie could really enhance your career. She comes from money, you know."

"I don't care if she has money or not! I'm not interested in messing around in my own backyard. That's just not good business."

"Well, I think she's perfect for you, and you should really give this some thought."

"Is there anything else you want to talk about?"

"No."

SCOTT walked out of the office and went down the hall, passing the hygiene room where Robin was working on a patient. He looked up when Scott walked by and winked at him. Scott smiled automatically, soothed by the knowledge that his redhead was so close. It was the only thing that would take away the sting of Ron's meddling.

He entered his office, locked the door behind him, and threw himself in his chair, spinning around so that he looked out the window at the view of the San Francisco harbor. He couldn't believe that Ron would suggest that he hook up with Susie for the sake of money. What the fuck! Was he eighteen and looked like he needed someone to set him up? The whole situation would be ludicrous if it weren't so pathetic.

He knew that it would be challenging, trying to blend his life with Ron Morris's, knowing full well what kind of person he was, but it would be *so* worth it in the end. This was a once-in-a-lifetime deal, and he knew it from the minute the papers were presented to him.

He remembered sitting in his office in Raleigh the first time he'd heard about the offer. Ron Morris, sole owner of a four-million-dollar practice was looking to sell out. It caught his eye as soon as his financial planner pointed it out, because he'd been looking to buy into something, and naturally, San Francisco called to him like a siren's song. He'd asked his lawyer to investigate and get more details about the man and his practice and was told that it was an opportunity he'd be foolish to pass up. He was also told a little bit about Ron's personality, but Scott pooh-poohed it away, thinking it was irrelevant. He'd deal with it as soon as he got to know Ron better. Surely no one who lived in San Francisco for so long could be as homophobic as his lawyer made Ron out to be.

Well, he was wrong, of course. Ron Morris was a throwback to the dinosaurs, firmly ensconced in his beliefs. Scott knew that his being openly gay would put the kibosh on the entire contract, and so he had made the decision to say nothing and virtually went into the closet he'd come out of years ago. The carrot dangled in front of him was too delicious to pass up. He'd be able to pay off all his student loans and settle into a guaranteed six-figure income without going through years of trying to establish a practice. He was first and foremost a practical man. He hadn't graduated Cum Laude for nothing. His long list of accomplishments only attested to how driven he was when it came to his career. He was not about to let the fact that he was gay stop him from succeeding.

Ron would never understand anything about his lifestyle nor did Scott care to try and win him over. It wasn't his business to show Ron the light. Scott had to stay focused on his eventual goals and get through this year somehow.

So he had kept to himself since his move to the Bay Area, never daring to venture out into the nightlife that he knew was out there. Whatever sporadic encounters he'd had in the last six months had been away from the city and always one-night stands; he couldn't risk any rumors getting back to Ron. He figured that nine more months of this lie would be worth the prize at the end. Once the papers were signed and his was the only name on the door, he'd come out. He was pretty confident in his professional abilities, knowing he was damn good at his job, and once the patients were used to him, they'd deal with whatever he was. He knew that most people were willing to let bygones be bygones, so long as his choices didn't impact their personal lives. Not everyone was a crusader like Ron.

But things had gotten a little more complicated with Robin appearing. Who knew that a chance encounter would turn into such an amazing relationship? He'd thought of nothing else since he and Robin had their first scene at his apartment last week. The man had him whipped, literally and figuratively, Scott thought, amused at his own play on words.

He closed his eyes, leaned back in his chair, pulled out his cock, and proceeded to do his homework. Robin had winked at him, the signal they'd established. Every time Robin winked at him, he had to go back to his office, lock the door, and pleasure himself to the brink of an orgasm, then pull back, submitting to his Master's wish to get him ready for the evening's session.

Chapter 7

"WHAT the hell!" Susie spat out. "Has Dr. Morris never heard of direct deposit?" She and Robin were standing in line waiting their turn for a teller at the Bank of America on Post Street. It was unbelievable that anyone in this day and age would deal with paper checks. Par for the course, she supposed. Everything else about her new boss was pretty archaic. Why should this be any different?

"I know… this is such a pain," Robin replied, glancing at his watch every few minutes. "All this waiting is eating into my lunch hour."

"I had errands to run," Susie said, tossing her hair and checking her phone for missed messages. "Now I'll be lucky if I have time for a quick bite."

"Why don't we talk to him?" Robin asked. "If we all agree on this, then maybe he'll be convinced to sign up."

"I doubt that it'll do any good. Have you noticed that he doesn't seem to belong to this century?"

"He's definitely old school."

"He's old, period. I wish he would just quit and let Scott take over."

"Scott?" Since when did an assistant call her boss by his first name?

"I've known Dr. Gregory for a while. We were at Northwestern together."

"Oh." Robin had no idea; in fact, there was a lot he didn't know about Scott.

"We trolled the bars and fought over dates."

"Did you?"

"Why do you look so surprised? I can be friends with him, even though he's gay, and my employer."

"Who said he was gay?" Jesus Christ! Did she know that he was a sub as well?

"Oh please, Robin… whatever game he's playing right now won't fly with me. I've known him far too long." Susie paused in the middle of her conversation and looked up at Robin. "You find him attractive, don't you?"

"Don't ask, won't tell."

She let out a quick laugh and hit him lightly on the arm. "I hope you don't think you have me fooled, too. I know my tits don't do a thing for you."

Robin smiled easily; glad it was all out in the open. "Hon, tits aren't my favorite thing, but if I were to ever switch sides, I'd definitely consider yours. Are they real?"

"Hell, yes!"

"Good for you!" Robin smiled down at her, comfortable with the vibes he was getting. She seemed genuinely nice, although a little high strung. She kept on scrolling through her messages.

"Didn't you say you were new in town?" he asked, letting his curiosity get the better of him.

"Yeah, I've only been here for about a month."

"Do you know a lot of people here?"

"Why?"

"You haven't stopped looking at your messages. That's a lot of mail for someone who's just moved."

Susie looked at Robin in surprise. "It's really none of your business."

"You're right, it's not. I'm sorry."

"Well, if you must know, I get messages everyday from my mother's caregiver."

"Oh, I'm sorry, hon. I'm a jerk for asking."

"It's all right."

"Why do they text you and not your father?"

"He's my stepfather, and he really couldn't be bothered. So long as he signs the check each month he feels like he's done his duty. They weren't married that long."

"How long were they married?"

"About five years."

"Oh. What about your real dad?"

"He's a big loser. Took off when I was four, and we haven't heard a word since."

"Nice."

"Hey, it is what it is. Can we get back to you and your issues?"

"What issues?"

"Do you have a thing for the boss?"

"What if I do?" He tried to sound casual, just another queer with the hots for a good-looking guy. It's not like she didn't already know Scott was gay, but how observant was she? Did she see how they were acting around each other, or was she just throwing this out to make conversation?

"Does he know?"

"What?"

"That you think he's hot!"

"No! And I'm not about to tell him, and neither should you."

"I won't. Your secret is safe with me; besides, this bit of information would seriously fuck up Dr. Morris, big time."

"It's not him I'd like to fuck."

"Uh-huh! You're jonesing for Scott, aren't you?"

"Well, look at him, for God's sake. He's like a poster boy for *The Young and the Beautiful*."

"He is pretty, but you're not his type."

"What's his type?"

"He and I have always been attracted to dark guys. We like Latinos, men with mixed blood… not redheads!" Susie laughed.

"Oh well."

"I think you're very cute, for whatever it's worth."

"Thanks, honey, but I'm doing just fine without your endorsement."

"Let's go cruising."

"What?"

"Let's go out tonight. I haven't gotten laid in weeks."

"I hardly think that being with me will get you laid."

"Please? I don't know anyone around here, and I really need to get some."

Where the heck did she think he was going to take her? He couldn't stroll into a BDSM club with Susie on his arm. "Have you heard of vibrators?"

"Robin, you're being a total ass."

"Sorry, hon, but I've already made plans."

"Can I come?"

"Not tonight. But I promise to take you out in the next few days, okay?"

"This sucks."

"Have you looked online?"

"I'm not into electronic dating. They're all a bunch of losers."

"Suz, don't despair… I promise we'll tour the town; how about Thursday?"

"This Thursday, as in the day after tomorrow?"

"Yes."

"Okay." She smiled, satisfied with his answer. "I can deal with that."

"Good, now move forward, it's your turn."

She stepped up to the teller for her transaction, and Robin observed her as she turned on the charm and did her thing. She really was a nice person, from the little he'd seen, and had an excellent work ethic. The lab was always spotless at the end of the day, and he knew Jenna had nothing to do with it. She was as burnt out as Dr. Morris, and now, with the addition of the two new people, she felt little guilt in leaving piles of dirty instruments and trays for Susie and him to clean up. The only time Jenna did anything was if Scott or Ron asked her to. She seemed to take a special interest in Scott and ignored Robin and Susie.

So far Susie's complaints had been muttered under her breath. He wondered how long it would be before she said something to Scott. She didn't strike him as being all that stoic. Then again, with this revelation about her mother, he realized that there was a side to Susie that he knew very little about; the caring daughter who seemed to eclipse the spoiled little rich girl she appeared to be.

He glanced at his watch again and saw that he still had a half hour; it was more than enough time to make the hardware run. He'd promised himself he'd buy some new equipment with his first paycheck, and he wanted to get the rings and pulleys for his initial caning scene with Scott. He'd yet to do that, putting it off for lack of proper equipment and space. But Scott had agreed to turn his spare room into their playroom, so Robin planned on working there tonight. He'd choose all the stuff they needed and pay for it. Scott could pick it up in his car on their way home from work.

It had been ten days since their first session. Since then they'd met two more times, and although each session had been great, Scott had not gotten into subspace. He was more than responsive, easily submitting to the flogging or spanking, but Robin felt he wasn't holding out long enough, that he was allowing his feelings to take over.

Being around Scott during the day changed the dynamic of the D/s relationship he was used to. In the past, he'd meet his scene partner for a session and then never see him again unless the other man asked for a second or third meeting. Because of his schooling and the fact that he wasn't into the club scene, he rarely had more than three sessions with the same guy. It had made it that much easier to distance himself and not let any emotions interfere with his dominant role.

He had been attracted to Scott before he even knew he was into the scene. There was a part of him that was very much interested in Scott the man, not so much the sub, although he knew it was both parts of Scott that made him so appealing.

But Dr. Gregory was keeping that part of himself under a tight watch. He was reluctant to share any information about his life, trying to maintain some semblance of control at work, since he would eventually become Robin's employer. The mere fact that he hadn't bothered to share their history with Susie was proof he was trying to separate his work and private life from their D/s relationship.

Robin had known from the beginning it was going to be different with him, he just didn't realize *how* different. He hadn't counted on falling this quickly and this hard. It had never happened before, so he was floundering right now, trying to get back some of the control he felt he was relinquishing.

It would be beneficial to them both if he could get Scott into subspace and pick up the dominance they both needed in order to continue with this side of their relationship. The other would have to just work itself out or fizzle out, whichever came first.

Robin hoped having the chains might do the trick. He almost wished he had access to a club and all the equipment, but he knew that it would never work, even if he could afford to join. Scott would never agree to go to such a public place for fear he'd be spotted.

So he had to improvise and get creative until he had all his gear. The mind games he played with Scott were wonderful tools to get him ready for their evening sessions. Scott was usually so strung out by the time they closed the door of his apartment, Robin would let him come immediately to take the edge off. After that, he'd have a pretty compliant sub who never failed to do what he asked, every response eager and willing; however, it wasn't what Robin or Scott hoped for. He wanted to push Scott to his limits, get him into the zone where his mind left him and the pain switched over to the perfect pleasure. Only then would Robin be satisfied.

The ringing of his phone snapped Robin out of his thoughts. It was his mother making her daily phone call.

"Mama."

"How's my favorite redhead?"

"Excellent! I got paid today."

"Woohoo! Good times, huh, sweet cakes?"

"Thank God! Maybe I can actually have a steak tonight."

"Robin, you know that you can always buy beans and tuna. They're cheap and a good source of protein."

"Ma, if I see another can of tuna, I'll hurl."

"I'm sorry, honey. I know it's been a rough few weeks for you."

"It's all over, Ma. I've gotten paid, and I'm flush. I'm sending you some dough."

"You don't need to."

"I want to, so shut up already."

"Thank you, hon. Are you going to be able to come and visit anytime soon?"

"Maybe. It'll depend on a few things."

"Is he blond or brunet?"

Robin laughed, so busted as usual. "He's blond and walks with the angels."

"Wow."

"Ma, he's fucking gorgeous."

"But is he good to you?"

"Ooh, yeah," Robin drawled, in his best imitation of the group, Yello.

"Okay. Stop right there, don't need to know more."

Robin laughed happily. He was in a great mood because he had money in his pocket and a man in his life. What more could he ask for?

"Ma, I've got to run."

"Okay, hon. Take care and be safe. I love you."

"Love you too. Watch your back."

"Always."

Robin found himself in front of Ace Hardware, and he raced inside to do the fastest shopping in the world. Fortunately, they had everything he needed. He paid for it and told the clerk he'd be by about five-fifteen to pick everything up. He looked at his watch once more and saw he had ten minutes left. He sprinted out of the store and up the hill to the office.

Chapter 8

AS soon as the doors of the apartment slammed shut, Scott started to strip off his clothes, leaving them in piles around him. He had his head bent, and he shook with want. He'd been thinking of this moment all day, and now that he and Robin were finally alone, he was lightheaded with anticipation. He'd almost come in the elevator when Robin kissed him suddenly and pressed his hand to his tented pants. When he finally stood naked in front of his master, his cock pointed rigidly away from his body.

"Is that for me, baby?"

"Please… would you get me off?" Scott begged in a voice that bordered on desperate. Robin had winked at him three times today, each signal sending him into his office to jerk off to the edge of an orgasm, which had now taken on the proportions of a giant storm looming darkly on the horizon.

Robin looked at Scott and decided, "No." As much as he craved Scott's cock in his mouth, he knew he had to do something different tonight or the ending would be the same: a failure to achieve subspace, and thus, a failure on his part as a Dom.

"No?" Scott asked in a panic. "But, Master… in the past—"

Robin bent forward, kissing the protest away. Scott responded eagerly, sucking on Robin's tongue and moaning softly. Robin pushed back reluctantly and said, "You have to trust me, baby."

Scott whimpered and stepped back, resuming the display position, his erection a painful reminder of his state of mind.

"Good boy." Robin spoke softly in a soothing voice, running his hands across Scott's chest, making little circles around his nipples and then twisting them sharply, listening to Scott hiss. He leaned toward the blond's ear and sucked on his lobe, trying to ignore the pull of his own erection and the urge to get down on his knees and take Scott in his mouth and hear him screaming as his cock pulsed hot liquid down his throat. He pushed away roughly and said, "I've been too easy on you. It's time to raise this up a notch."

"Whatever makes you happy, Master," Scott replied, trying to find the right place in his head after being caught off guard.

"Good… now, come with me to the playroom and help me set up the whipping station."

Robin picked up the package from Ace and turned quickly so Scott wouldn't see how badly he was affected by his presence. He proceeded into the other room, walking gingerly to accommodate the erection that rubbed against his pants. They got down to business immediately, pulling out portable drills and stud finders. Robin worked quickly, obviously having done this before. Scott assisted, passing equipment as Robin asked for it, and finally, when Robin gave the chains a tug and saw that they were secured to the rings he put up on the ceiling, he stepped back, satisfied.

"Go to the kitchen and get us some water. Do you need to use the bathroom first?"

"Yes, Master."

"Do it and come back to get ready."

Robin took off his shirt and wiped the sweat off his face and underarms. His body was boiling over with excitement, the anticipation of what he was about to do making him sweat like a pig. He supposed that he stank, but he really didn't care at this point, and he was pretty sure that Scott wouldn't either. He'd never known any man who wasn't turned on by the smell of another man in heat.

Scott came back with two bottles of water. He handed them both to Robin and went back to standing in the display position with his hands clasped behind him and his eyes looking down at the floor.

Robin reached into his bag of tricks, pulled out a black leather cock harness, and proceeded to tie it onto Scott's erection, which hadn't softened one bit. "This will keep you in check while I'm caning you. You will not come until I'm good and ready, if at all."

"Yes, Sir… please, Sir."

Robin gave a final tug on the leather strap, but not before he bent down and licked the moisture off the weeping, rosy head. Scott sighed and thrust forward.

"Don't!"

"Sir!"

"Behave yourself or this will not have a happy ending."

"Yes, Master."

Robin took black leather cuffs lined in fur and attached them to Scott's wrists. He walked him over to the side of the room where the chains were hanging down and attached each wrist to the hooks at the end of the chains. Scott's arms stretched above his head at a comfortable angle.

Robin bent down and cuffed Scott's ankles with the same type of fur-lined bindings and attached a spreader bar to his feet. He was now completely immobilized. "Are you comfortable?" Robin asked, running his hand over Scott's ass, which was twitching with anticipation, exciting Robin further.

"Yes, Master."

"Use your safe word if you have to. What is it?"

"Blue, Sir."

"Very well." Robin moved back and walked over to pull the cane out of his duffel bag. It was made of rattan and had a wicked sting when it landed. If the cane wasn't used properly, it could break skin easily. However, used correctly, it made lovely red marks that would last for days.

He raised his hand and brought the cane down quickly. It whistled through the air and landed on Scott's ass, making a white stripe that quickly turned pink and red immediately thereafter. Robin heard that quick intake of breath and a rattling of chains as Scott moved around, trying to get more comfortable. "Are you okay?"

"Yes, Master."

"We proceed, then." Robin raised his hand and brought the cane down again, landing a stripe close to the first one, but not covering it. He repeated this step a few more times until Scott's behind was covered with red stripes, making it look like an old-fashioned barber's pole. Scott's breathing had deepened, and he leaned his head on one arm. Sweat poured down his back and landed in the small dip just above his ass crack. Robin had to restrain himself from moving to him and licking him clean. He imagined burying his face into that sweaty body, inhaling every musky bit of him, and he adjusted himself quickly, squeezing his cock to try and curtail his reaction that was starting to get out of control. He moved closer to Scott and rubbed a warm hand over his ass, admiring the stripes and whispering softly into Scott's ear. "You are flawless."

"Thank you… please, Sir?"

"What is it?"

"May I come?"

"Not yet, baby. You haven't earned it."

Scott groaned and bent his head. "More then… let me prove myself."

Robin moved back, every breath a struggle as his arousal strangled him. He wanted nothing more than to free Scott and fuck him till he passed out, but he knew it would be that much sweeter if he remained steadfast. He lifted his hand once more and laid several more stripes on him, amazed at Scott's ability to take the pain. Most people buckled under a few swipes of a cane, yet he'd hit him at least nine times with no end in sight. Finally, he heard Scott let out a guttural moan that seemed different from the others. It was this last blow that acted as the spark, setting off the signal that switched the pain to the almost unbearable pleasure they were both seeking.

Robin's arousal leached out of him as surely as the drops of perspiration covering his body. He felt claustrophobic, bound by this terrible need closing in on him quickly, so he stepped out of his pants and tossed them aside, freeing up his cock, which now bobbed obscenely in front of him. He stood there naked, almost glowing with the force of his desire, and he raised his hand for one last time and caught Scott between his leg and his ass, as close to his balls as possible. The sound that came out of Scott's throat made Robin's hair stand on end. It was a ragged scream that came from some primal place deep within him. His head fell back and the muscles on his arms stood out in sharp relief as his body went slack and his eyelids fluttered. Robin knew he had him.

He moved up to Scott quickly and embraced him from behind. Scott leaned his dead weight on him as he floated in whatever subspace Robin had sent him. "I've got you, baby. Let it go."

"Master...."

Robin quickly unsnapped the bindings on Scott's wrists and the bar at his feet, laying him down on the floor gently. He removed the cock harness and held Scott, talking softly into his ear as he let him fly. Both of their sexes remained rigid, waiting in anticipation for a mouth or an ass to ease the suffering. Finally, Robin couldn't stand it any longer.

"Roll over, baby. I've got to have you."

"So good to me," Scott moaned, getting on his hands and knees, spreading wantonly. "Fuck me, Master, please...."

"Need your taste first," Robin announced. He spread Scott's ass cheeks with strong hands and bent down and attacked the soft pink skin around his hole, finally tasting him after craving this for the last hour. "Such a sweet boy...." He lapped gently.

"Master... please... oh, God, fuck me...."

Robin pulled away reluctantly, his eyes half-glazed with lust, staring at Scott who now leaned on his elbows with his head down. He'd spread his legs wider and lifted his ass higher, offering himself in complete submission, ready for whatever Robin had in store for him.

"Master," Scott pleaded, almost at the end of his rope.

"Now, baby," Robin said, grabbing the condom and the lube, readying himself in seconds. He pulled Scott up with both hands on his hips and breached him forcefully, listening as their dual screams reverberated in the small room.

"Say it for me, baby." Robin huffed, barely able to control his breathing as he thrust in and out. "Say you're my whore!"

"Yes… oh, God, yes… your whore… yes… oh, fuck, so good… yours, Master!"

"My slut, my baby, oh my God," Robin growled as he pulled Scott hard against him, thrusting forcefully, shifting angle until he hit the gland that made Scott scream while he reached around and wrapped his long fingers around Scott's distended shaft and tugged until he felt the hot liquid pouring out of him in a steady stream as his own orgasm caught up and he released into the condom, much too soon for his liking.

"Master…." Scott's voice was barely discernible as he collapsed, his arms and legs giving out completely.

Robin pulled out and tossed the condom aside. He rolled Scott over and bent down to suckle his half-hard cock, tasting the cum that still coated the bulbous head, and Robin devoured the sweetness, licking him clean as he listened to the sounds coming out of his throat, each sigh and whimper opening doors to Robin's heart that had been closed all his life. He moved up to Scott's face and kissed his mouth, sucking on his lower lip and running his tongue gently around his teeth and gums.

"Master… I'm flying high…."

"I know, baby."

"You were wonderful," Scott whispered, his body and voice shaky with emotion. "So masterful and strong."

Robin was practically incoherent, completely caught up in his sub's success tonight. He knew he was far more emotional than he should be so early in the game. It was his job as Dom to maintain control over the situation and not give into his feelings, but his heart seemed to have its own agenda.

"Master?"

"Yes?"

"Did I make you happy?" Scott's eyes were closed as he lay in Robin's arms, so he didn't see the tears trickling down his master's cheek, but he did hear a new word that answered his question.

"You did, my love."

"Your love?"

"My love."

Chapter 9

ROBIN looked out on the dance floor, catching a glimpse of Susie as she moved sensuously in front of the poor schmuck who'd dared to ask her to dance. She showed no mercy as her lower body undulated gracefully, driving the poor man nuts. Robin hoped the guy had whatever he needed to keep up with her tonight, as she seemed determined to end up in someone's bed.

He'd made good on his promise to take her dancing, letting her drag him into a straight club for the first time in ages. It was just as well, since he didn't plan on hooking up with anyone.

His head was still caught up in the session he'd had with Scott two nights ago. They had talked about it briefly, dwelling on the physical aspects of subspace, but skirting around the emotional impact of the encounter. Neither man seemed interested in discussing the fact that both of them had crossed over to another level in their relationship.

Robin knew he and Scott should make the commitment and sign a contract for at least six months. It was a first for him, and he knew that it would be a first for Scott as well; however, he didn't think it was a good idea to continue on without it. They were getting in too deep, and he had other things to take into consideration, such as his job.

If things went south with them, it would be awkward and probably force him into leaving to find another position, something he wasn't too keen on doing.

Scott seemed to have retreated into his head so Robin had left him alone for the last two days. He hadn't winked at him or made any overtures to get together after work. It was almost as if they were afraid to repeat the depth of the emotional level they'd achieved that one time, because it would only open up the floodgates, forcing them to acknowledge their feelings.

Robin was honest enough to admit he was falling in love with Scott at a terrifying speed. His submission was a thing of beauty, as was his physical person, a very difficult combination to ignore. Mentally, he was a wonderful challenge, pushing Robin to places he longed for but could never achieve for lack of money and education. Scott talked to him about dentistry and his cases as if he were a peer, not just a hygienist. He assumed Robin could keep up, never underestimating him in the least bit.

And despite the fact he was earning a huge salary, Scott was unassuming and respectful to all the employees, never pulling his weight or acting like a prima donna. He was never late. He stayed until the last person left the office and always made it a point to greet everyone in the morning and at night, just because he was a nice guy. The patients loved him, as well as all the referring dentists who'd come into contact with him.

Susie's appearance in front of him interrupted his thoughts of Scott.

"Get me a drink, will you?"

"Sure, hon. What do you want?"

"A frozen margarita with lots of salt."

"Coming right up," he told her as he moved off to the bar. He wondered what had become of her dance partner. She probably scared him away.

He couldn't figure out why someone so beautiful and so rich could be unattached at her age. Was it the fact that she was so independent that scared men away, or did she deliberately push them out of her life once she'd had her fill?

He'd have to quiz Scott on what made Susie tick, for no other reason than he cared. She was sweet, and he wanted to try and help her find the love connection she seemed to disdain so much. He'd spent some time earlier this evening going over her theories on men and their lack of staying power in her life. He'd never met a girl with her mindset. It was kind of refreshing in a way, sort of like being with another gay man who was constantly on the prowl looking for his trick of the night, but in her case, it was the man of her fantasy.

Robin teased her and told her she should try a woman for a change, just to see if maybe that's what she was looking for. The horror on her face made him crack up with laughter, appreciating the fact that she wanted nothing to do with anyone that didn't have a working cock. Dildos didn't count, as far as she was concerned.

"Here's your drink, hon. Where's Mr. Universe?"

"He's probably in the restroom jerking off."

"What did you say to him?"

"That I planned on sitting on his face for a good hour."

Robin laughed and asked, "Are you for real or is this all an act?"

"I'd challenge you, except I know you'd rather eat glass than fuck a woman."

He grabbed her and hugged her tightly against his body. "I swear to God, if I ever have a hankering for snatch, you'll be at the top of the list."

"I don't suppose you've hooked up with anyone here?" Susie asked, sipping her drink.

"Nah… this is breeder central, hon. It'd be like trying to find a clean pig in a mud bath."

"Are you saving yourself?" she asked with a wicked smile. "I could probably put a little bug in Scott's ear, tell him you're interested."

"Don't even go there, girlfriend. The boss is off limits for me."

"Oh, you're no fun at all, Robin. Think of all the endless scenarios."

"Scenarios that could get us both fired, if Dr. Morris ever found out."

"Speaking of Morris," Susie interrupted, "you won't believe what he said to me the other day."

"What?"

"He thinks that Scott and I would make a great couple."

"Couple of what?"

"Exactly!" Susie burst out laughing. "He has no idea what he's talking about."

"Hold on… you mean a couple, as in, man and woman kind of couple?"

"Uh huh. He thinks we'd make the perfect pair. The doctor and his built-in wife-slash-assistant. What could be better?"

"He's got issues."

"Ya think?"

"Seriously. Does Scott, I mean, Dr. Gregory, does he know what's going on?"

"I haven't had a chance to tell him yet. He'll probably shit when he hears this," Susie said, draining the rest of her drink. "You know that he had a huge falling out with his parents when he came out."

"No."

"Well, he did. I happened to be around, since it was when we were in Chicago together. They made his life miserable, threatened to pull their financial support if he didn't get his act together."

"So what did he do?"

"He stepped back into the closet for a while, until he got his financial aid in place. Then he told them to fuck off."

"I see… so what he's doing now, this denial for Morris's sake isn't anything new."

"Not really. He's done this once before."

"Interesting. Well, get a move on, girlie. You're date's back."

"Okay. Listen, Robin. You can leave if you want. I'm probably going to drag this guy home with me."

"You sure?"

"Yeah."

Robin pulled out his phone and said, "Give me your number and take mine while you're at it. I want you to call me later, just to let me know that you're okay and he's not some weirdo serial killer."

"You're so sweet."

"I'm just worried about my new fag hag."

Susie smiled up at him, grabbed his phone, and started keying in numbers.

He left after that, walking out of the club and going underground to catch the train back up to where he lived. He'd rented an apartment about eight blocks from work, simply because he didn't have a car and hated dealing with rush hour commuters. This way he could walk back and forth and not have to worry about wheels.

It wasn't the best neighborhood in the world, with borderline hookers and crackheads. He was close to the mission district, but not quite. Very close to the Castro area, but still many streets and paychecks away. He and his mother had lived in far worse, so this was a step up for him, especially since it was his very own place. The fact that he didn't have to share his living space with undesirables or vermin made it that much nicer.

When he got to his apartment, he realized it wasn't that late. It was only eleven o'clock, so he decided to try and finish up unloading the few boxes he'd been ignoring since his move. These contained books, and he really had nowhere to put them until now. He'd bought himself some bricks and planks of wood the other day at the same hardware store where he'd bought his chains, and he'd created a makeshift bookcase he started to fill as neatly as possible. By the time he was done unloading and putting everything on the new shelves, it was time for bed.

His phone rang, surprising because of the hour. It was almost midnight.

"Susie?"

"No… it's Scott."

"Oh, is anything wrong?"

"I can't sleep. Were you out with Susie?"

"Yeah. I took her dancing, but we parted ways over two hours ago, which reminds me, she still hasn't called to check in."

"Did you ask her to?"

"Yup."

"She will, she's very responsible."

"Okay. Is there anything I can do for you?"

"You can come over."

"Now?"

"Yes."

"I don't think it's a good idea, love. We need to talk first."

"Let's talk then."

"At midnight, on a Saturday?"

"When else? It's not like we have a lot of time or privacy during the week." Scott said, with a hint of desperation in his voice.

"This is true."

"I'll pick you up… I'd rather you didn't take a cab. Is that all right?"

Robin rubbed his eyes and sighed into the phone. "I'm not up to doing a scene tonight."

"No scenes. Just talking, okay? You and me, not Master and sub."

Robin caved. "All right." He hung up and went to the bathroom to wash his face and brush his teeth. He looked in the mirror above his sink and saw that he needed a haircut. His hair was curling around his neck, flipping out as it tended to do when it got too long. He'd have to make a trip out to see his mom, who'd been cutting his hair all his life. He didn't trust anyone else with it.

His phone rang just as he was leaving the apartment to wait downstairs.

"Robin?"

"Yeah, hon?"

"I'm fine—"

"He still there?"

"Snoring beside me."

"Well, two hours of sex would wear anyone out. Are you good or more importantly, was he?"

"It's fine. I'll talk to you tomorrow, okay?"

"Good night, Suz."

"Night."

Chapter 10

THEY drove up Van Ness Avenue in silence; the only sound was the quiet purr of the engine as they headed toward Jackson Street and Scott's apartment.

"You should think about moving, Robin." Scott was a little surprised that Robin lived deep in the downtown area, almost on the fringes of the tenderloin district.

"It's close to work, and I didn't know any better when I got here," Robin explained. "It's also affordable, and I can certainly take care of myself. Believe me, I've seen a lot worse."

"Did you sign a lease?"

"Six months."

"Well, you have five months to look around. Surely you can find something close to work in a better neighborhood."

"We'll see," Robin said quietly. If Scott knew what kind of shithole he'd grown up in, he'd realize this location wasn't that bad.

They got to the apartment building, and Scott hit the remote that gave them access to the underground parking. He left the vehicle in his reserved spot, and they made their way to the elevator. Scott was in blue jeans and a 49ers sweatshirt. His hair looked soft and clean as it fell in a silky curtain on his forehead. Robin admired his ass as he walked behind him. The faded jeans fit tightly around his perfect butt, and the mental picture of Scott on his hands and knees made Robin groan as his cock filled quickly. *So much for good intentions....*

The apartment was warm, and there was music coming through the speakers. It wasn't quite elevator music, but close; a soft jazzy kind of sound that wasn't familiar to Robin, but was soothing nonetheless. The door had no sooner closed when Scott pushed Robin gently against it and kissed him on the mouth, moaning softly as he did so.

"I thought we weren't playing tonight?"

"We're not," Scott replied, breathless. "I just wanted to kiss you."

"Kissing is good," Robin answered, pulling Scott tightly against his torso and resuming the kisses that started to get deeper and hotter. "I've wanted to do this for the last two days."

"I know," Scott breathed, pulling away from Robin and looking him in the eye. "Would you consider having sex outside of a scene? No D/s scenario, just us?"

"I don't know if I can separate one from the other."

"Can we try?" Scott almost begged.

"All right," Robin said seriously, "but we'll do it in your room, not the playroom."

He nodded, and then he held Robin's hand and pulled him gently toward the master bedroom. There were fake logs burning in the corner fireplace that cast a glow on the darkened room. They moved toward it and continued the kissing that had been interrupted on their way into this private sanctuary. Scott slowly peeled off Robin's clothes, taking care to be gentle and not rush. He wanted to do this right, to try and figure out where they were going in this relationship. He'd always been on the receiving end of Robin's passion; tonight, he wanted to give, to orchestrate the events and show Robin how much he cared, because he did. Desperately.

"Let me make love to you," Scott's voice was gruff, filled with an emotion that had only come forward that one time while he was in subspace. When Robin made no move to contradict him, he was encouraged, and he continued disrobing him until Robin was naked.

Scott looked at him as if it were the first time, because the reality was that although they'd had sex many times, he'd always played the submissive keeping his eyes downcast. He'd never really had a chance to scrutinize Robin's naked body, and so he did, admiring every inch of the lean, muscular form. Robin's arms and legs were covered with a layer of soft hair the color of peaches at the bottom of a homemade pie, a wonderful mix of browns and oranges and spun sugar that made up the unique color. His hair sprung out in rich curls, longer than when they'd first met, the ringlets seemingly tighter and more abundant as Scott ran his hands through the heavy mass. He lowered his eyes to Robin's cock which was half-hard, nestled in the soft reddish-brown hair. It was thick and long and worked superbly well as Scott recalled the feel of it filling him on more than one occasion. There were drops of moisture dotting the plump head, begging to be licked up, and he would, in just a minute, as soon as he'd finished admiring the whole package. Robin looked like a painting of a Viking that Scott had seen somewhere, some majestic virile man with a fur vest standing beside his horse in a battle scene. All he needed was the horned helmet and the blood streaks on his cheek to complete the picture.

"Whoever put your colors together did a wonderful job," Scott said, continuing with his scrutiny.

Robin smiled, pleased that Scott thought he was good-looking. "My mother is also a redhead, although she's a bit more muted."

"I'd like to meet her someday and thank her."

"She'd like that." Robin replied, never moving from his spot. He waited for Scott to make all the moves tonight, afraid to be the aggressor and disturb this new experience.

"I want to call you Red when we're in this mode, when it's just the two of us without the whips. May I?"

"Yes, if you'll let me call you, Scott."

"I sort of liked 'love' better."

"That's a given—"

"Am I?"

"What?" Robin knew what he was asking; he just didn't want to say it out loud.

Scott moved to him and held his face with both hands, looking into the blue eyes that were old and had seen so much despite the youth of the body they occupied. "Am I your love?"

Robin's composure shattered, and he whispered "Yes" before he could stop himself.

Scott kissed him fiercely, invading his mouth with an aggressive tongue, attacking every part of the wet cavern, whimpering when Robin met his every thrust taunting him right back.

"I want you to lie down," Scott said, taking Robin's hand and leading him to the queen-sized bed. He started pulling off his clothes as they made their way, scattering them all over the room. He pulled off his jeans, finally, only to reveal his naked self that caused Robin to groan mournfully. "You are fucking killing me with this commando routine of yours."

"I can't help it, Red. I hate waiting, hate underwear, and hate being confined."

"So much hate," Robin said with a grin. He stopped and waited for Scott to catch up to him. "Isn't there anything you love?"

"You."

"Scott—"

"It's true, but please don't say anything right now. Let's just go with it, okay?"

"Okay."

They lay on the bed facing each other, two men at the height of their beauty. "I could look at your face for hours," Scott whispered, "but right now, I'm dying to make love to you, to do wicked things to your body with my tongue. Master, may I?"

Robin flashed a quick grin and said, "Yes, you may."

Scott started with Robin's neck, littering him with soft, wet kisses, laving him around his ears and switching to his shoulder blades, moving down his torso, paying special attention to the light brown coins that puckered in response to his magical tongue as it flicked over them. The wet trail continued its downward path, stopping momentarily to dip into his belly button and tease Robin mercilessly, finding out that this was a spot to come back to in the future as his lover writhed underneath him, babbling incoherent words that only goaded him.

Scott stopped when he arrived at his destination, swiping his hot tongue on the rosy pink head glistening with slippery drops of dew.

"Oh God." Robin groaned, as soon as he felt himself engulfed in Scott's warm mouth. "Jesus Christ," he cried out as he felt the sucking motion, the intense pull that was making him a little crazy. He fisted Scott's hair, twisting the strands around his clenched fingers, lifting his hips up higher, hoping to get in deeper, rewarded by Scott's amazing throat as it swallowed him without hesitation, milking his cock with undulating muscles.

"Fuck, fuck, oh my God!"

Scott never stopped; he kept on doing his thing, and Robin pushed him away forcefully because he didn't want to come yet, wanted to drag this out as long as possible. "Stop... please, love."

"Aren't you enjoying it?"

The sight of Scott at his groin looking up at him with disheveled hair and a mouth plump and wet with passion made Robin groan again. "Too much... I want to last longer."

"Red?"

"What, love?"

"I want...."

"Yes?"

Scott didn't answer but bent down instead, forging ahead with his plan, not giving Robin the chance to say no. He pushed Robin's knees up, shoving his legs apart so he could attack the soft pink skin surrounding his beautiful hole, and he was rewarded by his Master crying out, "Scott… Jesus… oh my love…."

"Feel it, Red," Scott answered, pausing for just one second to add, "feel my love," he whispered, going back to destroying his lover in little bits as he suckled on the soft skin of his perineum and lapped at his asshole until Robin was twitching and moaning uncontrollably. Scott rolled him over, waiting to feel the resistance, but there was none as Robin lay on his stomach, panting with desire.

Robin heard the foil rip and the lube pop open, but when he felt the cold liquid he finally snapped out of his trance and said, "No!"

"Please," Scott begged, holding Robin down as he twisted around violently.

"No! I don't switch," Robin said in a panic, losing his erection as he struggled to regain control of the situation. He sat up and looked at Scott, wild with fear, wanting to apologize but never actually saying the words. "I can't, Scott. It's not who I am."

Scott realized his error quickly, and he handed Robin the condom and the lube, bending forward and kissing him on the mouth, "Whatever makes you happy, Master. I wanted to please you, but if fucking me is all that you want, then do it."

"Scott."

"Please? I need you inside me now," Scott insisted, trying to diffuse the whole situation and getting Robin's head back into sex, forgetting that he'd automatically slipped into the whole D/s scenario.

They kissed again, and Robin tried to relax, to get back into the moment, but it was spoiled and not quite the same. He tugged at himself, watching his cock come back to life, and he rolled the condom on automatically, spreading the lube over his shaft and Scott, who waited patiently on his hands and knees, assuming the position, showing his submission to the lover who'd turned back into a Dom in a split second.

Robin entered him, closing his eyes tight, aware of the tears that fought to pour out of him, but he blinked them back and found his place in his head again, fucking the hell out of his submissive until they both came in a shuddering mess.

Chapter 11

SCOTT was having lunch at his desk today instead of leaving the building as he normally would. The last surgery had run over the allotted time, and his next patient was due in about thirty minutes, which only left enough time for a quick bite of the sandwich that Jenna bought for him. He was surprised when she walked in with the sandwich, solicitous of his needs. She'd been doing that a lot lately, making sure he was comfortable and well cared for during the day.

He barely tasted the turkey and cheese, chewing and swallowing automatically to provide fuel to a body that needed the sustenance. He'd never been into food, unlike many of his friends who rhapsodized over restaurants and new dishes they'd tried. He'd always eaten to live, not the other way around.

His obsessions were darker and harder to discuss in polite society. The sting of a cane or the whack of a paddle was his favorite thing. He couldn't care less about wines and cuts of meat. He cared about makers of bullwhips and floggers; the type of leather used to create these instruments of torture that turned him on and where to buy them. That was one side of him, the darker side that he kept close to his chest.

The other side of his personality was all about healing, discipline, and structure, along with the trappings that money and success could buy. This overachiever side of his personality had made him compromise over the years, pushing aside his personal life and his submissive tendencies to become successful so that he no longer depended on his parents or anyone else. Falling into this deal with Ron was a godsend in many ways. It had given him the opportunity to shoot to the top of the list, bypassing the years of struggle most men his age had to endure. The fact that he was living a lie was irrelevant for now. He was focused on his ultimate goal of buying into the practice, and he would do or say whatever was necessary to achieve it.

Robin—or Red, as he thought of him in private—was a complication he hadn't anticipated. The hunger that crept into Red's eyes when Scott would cry out in pain was empowering yet weakening in many ways. Knowing that his Dom was receiving the ultimate pleasure from his surrender set him on fire. The look on Red's face when he watched Scott submit was enough to make his knees weak and his cock swell. They fed each others' needs in the most primal way, deriving satisfaction from every encounter.

And it was this satisfaction that seemed to be crossing over to the other side, overflowing into his business world, to the rational part of his brain, making him say and do things he shouldn't. It was enough to dare him to take chances he normally wouldn't, such as calling Robin into his office for no reason other than a touch or a quick kiss. Scott was careless whenever Robin was around, lingering over patients who had already been checked just so he could stay in the room and look at him. He'd brush his hands when they passed instruments, feel the heat licking his cheeks as they touched. He would get hard just thinking about Red's hands twisting his nipples, biting his shoulder, and yanking on his hair as he drove into him, thrusting roughly into his ready ass. Visions of his Dom in full arousal would make him groan out loud, sometimes in the middle of a surgery, and Susie would look at him and wonder what was wrong.

He squirmed in his chair, feeling the butt plug pressing into him. Red had insisted that he wear it at work, another test of his submission. The pressure on his rectum was intense, keeping him in a state of high arousal, his mind constantly on his Master. He pushed back on the chair, lifting his hips as he squeezed his cock, willing it to quiet down, but it seemed to have a mind of its own, which was exactly what Red intended. He planned on keeping Scott excited all day so that he'd have him eating out of his hand by the time they closed the door of his apartment.

Scott picked up the phone and asked the receptionist if Robin had left for lunch. "No, he's in the staff room."

"Will you tell him I need him for a minute?"

"Sure thing, Doc."

He heard the knock, and the door pushed open, and Robin stood there with a wicked grin on his face. "You rang?"

"Oh God!"

His smile turned into a soft laugh as he shut the door behind him and locked it purposefully, moving quickly to stand in front of Scott's chair. He caressed Scott's face and lifted his chin before he kissed him, running his tongue hungrily around Scott's lips, listening to him whimper with want. "What is it, my love?"

"Please—"

"This will only make it that much better tonight."

"Master, I beg you...."

Robin pushed his scrubs down and unleashed his cock, as stiff as a prepubescent boy's, and he said, "Pull your zipper down."

Scott never took his eyes off Robin's engorged member, fumbling at himself as he freed his cock and held it tightly with his right hand.

"I want you to watch me pleasure myself," Robin whispered, in a voice now heavy with lust. "Don't come until I tell you."

"Master... please."

"Watch me, my love, and then I'll watch you."

Robin sat on the edge of the desk with his body in front of Scott, who'd moved his chair back to give Robin some space. Robin's hands were powerful and large, working hands that had brought Scott to climax on many occasions, but now he caressed his cock gently, running his thumb around the swollen head that was dotted with beads of pre-cum that Scott was dying to lick.

"Master... let me taste you!"

"No, love, watch me and play with yourself."

Scott kept his eyes on Robin, who began to pull and tug in earnest, moaning as his orgasm climbed easily from his curled toes to his distended cock. "Are you watching, my love?"

"Yes...." Scott was almost incoherent.

"I'm going to come all over my hand, let you lick my fingers clean."

"Yes... oh, God... yes."

Robin tugged a final time until he came in a rush, spurting drops of white into his hand which he used as a protective shield to prevent a big mess on his uniform.

"Master...." Scott begged in a voice that rose in desperation, his body writhing in discomfort. Robin took pity on him and allowed him to lick his fingers, watching his sub lapping at him, savoring his taste like a cat with the richest cream. Robin wrapped his other hand around Scott's beautiful cock and held it tightly, fisting it while he looked Scott in the eye and said, "Come for me, my love."

Scott cried out when he shot, missing Robin by an inch as he steered clear of the spray, but he moved back almost immediately, settling himself in between Scott's legs. He knelt down to take Scott's half-erect cock in his mouth, and he sucked on the residue, milking every last drop of him while Scott leaned his head back on the leather headrest and drew in ragged breaths as the pleasure raced through him.

"Master... thank you."

Robin looked up, his blue eyes brimming with something other than power and dominance, and said, "That was a gift from me, not your Master."

"Red—"

"Love." Robin caressed Scott's lips with his thumb and stood abruptly, "I have to go back to work." He pulled his pants up and walked out the door, leaving a confused and boneless Scott to get his act together, a feat in and of itself since the butt plug thrummed inside him, making him relive his orgasm over and over.

Scott squeezed his eyes tightly, aware that a piece of his heart had just left the room. He pulled tissues out of the box on his desk and quickly cleaned up the come that had landed on the carpet just as he heard the knock on the door.

Susie poked her head in. "I'm ready for you in room four."

"I'll be right there."

THE rest of the afternoon passed quickly in surgery. It was another case of a fractured tooth that needed to come out. No one had simple extractions anymore. These days it was always followed by a bone graft to prepare the site for a future implant. Sometimes they could put the implant in right away, but more often than not, they'd have to prepare the extraction site by debriding it and bone grafting with a combination of bovine and synthetic bone to create the healthy environment necessary to accept the titanium screw. It was almost a miracle, creating bone where there was nothing before in an area eaten away by bacteria and infection and then coming back a few months later when the bone had grown hard and healthy and place the implant. It was no wonder most baby boomers opted for this in lieu of the dreaded dentures that plagued their parents.

He completed the procedure, and after dispensing the usual prescriptions and instructions, he dismissed the patient and made his way back to his office. There was a note on his desk from Robin. "Off to visit my mother for a few days. I'll see you on Monday."

He sat down abruptly, letting a squeak escape his lips as the butt plug dug in deeper. He couldn't believe Robin would just leave without letting him know ahead of time. Granted, it was Friday and the perfect time to do it, but Scott was devastated, having looked forward to their session tonight like a drug addict hoping for a fix.

He ripped the note to shreds and tossed it in the trash, accompanied by a litany of curses. He then went into the bathroom and pulled out the butt plug, washed it efficiently and put it in his duffel bag. He wasn't going to suffer needlessly; not if he wasn't getting any kind of reward tonight. He made his way out of the bathroom, already dressed in street attire: a collarless long sleeved T-shirt and a pair of khakis with rubber-soled Merrills. Ron Morris stood in the middle of the room, dressed to go home as well. "Scotty, my man, I'm taking you out for dinner."

"You are?"

"Sure, why not? It's the end of a great month, and we need to celebrate. You game?"

Scott had no wish to go out with Ron, but since the object of his desire seemed to have skipped town, he gave in. "What did you have in mind?"

"You like Chinese?"

"Who doesn't?"

"There's this great place I know. We can walk there."

"I'm aware," Scott said, immediately thinking of Red and their first date. He was still angry that he'd left to visit his mother. Scott thought they had a better understanding. No matter what Red said about caring for him, there was a part of him that he still had not shared, which was probably the result of all the mixed signals Scott was sending out: one minute a sub and the next minute an employer, guarded and distant. Their situation was complicated and disturbing, dishonest in many ways because of this need to maintain the public persona. Maybe Red's departure was his way of saying he wanted out. Maybe it was time for some honesty, but Scott was afraid to disturb the fragile equilibrium for fear of losing him.

THE bus ride out to San Ramon took longer than he thought it would. It was around nine at night by the time Robin put the key in the lock at his mother's place. She'd left a plate for him in the refrigerator with a note telling him she'd be home around ten. He saw that she'd made him a taco casserole, the Mexican lasagna of sorts, layers of tortilla, cheese, salsa, and ground beef that he loved. He threw the plate in the microwave and waited a few minutes for it to warm up. When that was done, he sat down at the small kitchen table and inhaled the food. He rinsed out his plate and fork and then went to sit in front of the TV. He must have dozed off because the next thing he was aware of was his mother bending down to kiss his cheek.

"What time did you get in?" she asked, running her fingers through his red mane.

"What time is it?"

"Ten-ish."

"I've been here for about an hour or so."

"Did you eat?"

"Yes. Thanks for leaving me some dinner."

"You're welcome, honey. I'm going to bed, okay? I'm really tired tonight."

"You need help?"

"No."

Robin watched as she hobbled down the hallway. Her movements seemed more awkward than normal, the bump on her back more noticeable. She was leaning to one side from the severe curvature of her spine, the scoliosis wreaking havoc on her body as she got older. It made Robin sick to see her in so much pain, but this was the body she'd been born with, and she never complained. Denise just took it all with a grain of salt and made the best of it. Her one joy in life was sitting in her living room; living proof that doctors didn't always know what they were talking about. She was told she could never have kids because her pelvis was malformed and would never accommodate a child, yet she'd proved them wrong—almost killing herself at the end, but the resulting prize was so worth it.

"Mama?" Robin called out to her at the last minute, the rush of tenderness clutching at his throat.

"What, honey?"

"I love you."

"Love you too."

Chapter 12

"AND I really feel that you should consider dating Susie," Ron said, stuffing half a pot sticker in his mouth. "She's very attractive, don't you think?" he continued to talk through a mouthful of food.

Scott groaned inwardly, tired of hearing this for the third time tonight. He didn't know how else to say it, but he tried once more. "I'm not interested in dating her, Ron. We're friends, nothing else."

"How do you plan on buying the practice? Do you have money saved? Do you think you can get financing with all your outstanding student loans?"

"How do you know about my student loans?" Scott asked, angered by this apparent invasion into his financial portfolio.

"Did you think I wouldn't investigate you before I offered the deal?"

"Well, I assumed you'd review all my credentials. I didn't think you'd run a credit check."

"Scott," Ron said, pointing his chopsticks at him, "I need to make sure you're financially solvent. I don't want to waste my time with someone who can't cough up the money at the end of the contract."

"I wouldn't enter into this agreement if I didn't think I could come up with the cash."

"And here's my point, young man. Why borrow the money from a bank or your parents, when you can marry Susie and have it handed over to you?"

"I would never borrow the money from my parents. They don't have it, for one thing, and I would never put them in that kind of a position, for another."

"Whatever," Ron mumbled, waving the chopsticks again like he was swatting a fly. "You need to start thinking like a businessman, Scott, not some romantic, looking for true love."

Scott had just about reached the end of his fun level for the night. If Ron said one more word, he'd punch his lights out. He was already in a shitty mood because of Robin's sudden exodus and listening to Ron's grand scheme was getting on his last nerve. He was about to tell him to fuck off when the door of the restaurant opened, and a gay couple walked in with their arms around each other. Ron saw them and scowled, "Fucking queers. They're everywhere these days. I can't even have a meal without them in my face flaunting their sick love."

"They're not hurting anyone," Scott said coldly.

"They're sick!"

"Just drop it, Ron."

"Why? You think it's okay to be that way?"

"I think it's none of our business. What they do behind closed doors is private and not your concern."

"Well, you're wrong, Scott. It is my concern. Any God-fearing Christian should make it their concern. They are turning marriage into a farce."

Scott stood abruptly and said, "Ron, you're entitled to your opinion, but that doesn't mean I have to agree with you. It's not my wish to butt heads with you over this matter, so I think we should end this conversation right now. I'm afraid I have to go. Thank you for dinner."

"What?" Ron sputtered, looking up at Scott, shocked that he was leaving. "We're not done yet."

"Yes, we are. I'll see you on Monday."

Scott walked out of the restaurant in a rage. He would have cheerfully upturned the table just to see the look on Ron's face when the soup splashed all over him. However, it wouldn't have changed his mind or solved anything, so Scott took off and hoped that by the time he saw Ron again he'd have gotten over his anger at being left to finish his dinner by himself.

He got into his car and headed out of Chinatown, making his way up California Street toward home. He got stuck behind a cable car that was trudging up the hill and packed with tourists. By the time he was able to get around them, he decided to call Susie and ask her to go out with him tomorrow night. He could use a friend; someone who really knew him, besides, the thought of spending two nights by himself filled him with sadness.

ROBIN woke up to the smell of freshly brewed coffee and the sight of Denise puttering around in the kitchenette. He'd slept on the sofa since the one-bedroom apartment had no spare bed. He yawned and stretched, twisting around to work out the kinks before sitting up and taking the cup of coffee that was handed to him.

"Thanks," he acknowledged, sipping the hot brew slowly. They were both silent as they enjoyed their first cup, Denise's mind on what she had planned for the day, and Robin's on what he'd left behind in San Francisco. He ran his hands through his tangled locks and sighed, his morning boner a sure reminder of Scott. He stood up and made his way into the bathroom. "I need a haircut," he announced as soon as he got back to his position on the sofa.

"I see that," she smiled. "Is that why you're here?"

"Among other things."

"Are we going to talk about him, or shall we dance around the subject for a while and discuss my health?"

Robin grinned and said, "It's not fair."

"What?"

"That you can read my mind the way you do."

"Honey, I'd better be able to read your mind after twenty-seven years, or I'd flunk the mother-of-the-year award."

He laughed gently and moved to wrap his arms around her, squeezing tight. "How is your health?"

"Same old, same old. I wish I could get into my skin to oil my joints. I feel like I need a good lube job."

"I'd be careful with that last phrase, Ma," Robin teased.

"You're a pervert!"

He chuckled and said, "I'm your perv, so deal with it!"

She stood up and refilled her cup, bringing the coffee pot over to top off Robin's. Finally, when they were both settled again she asked, "What's his name?"

"Scott," he groaned, throwing his head back on the sofa and closing his eyes.

"That's a nice name, sort of yuppie."

"He is."

"You've fallen for a straight-laced yuppie?" Denise was a little surprised. Robin had always hung around with the racier, bad-boy types. Men in leather had been his preferred companions, and even though they'd never talked about his role in the BDSM world, she knew what was what.

"So, what's the problem?"

"He's my boss."

"Oh fuck," Denise said, softly.

"No shit."

"Honey, you need to back off."

"I didn't know he was my boss when we first hooked up!" Robin quickly spoke in his defense. "It's this really bizarre set of events, like some cosmic joke on both of us."

"But now you know, honey." Denise reached for Robin's hand and squeezed it gently. "It's not good to poop in your own backyard."

Robin groaned, the misery apparent in his deep blue eyes.

"Are you in love with him?"

"I guess… I don't know, Ma. I've never been in love before."

"Never?"

"I've never felt this way about anyone." Robin got off the sofa and went to get more coffee. "You got anything to eat?"

"There are English muffins with raisins and some yogurt."

"Negative on the yogurt, but I'll have a muffin." He took one out of the box in the fridge and popped it in the toaster. "You want one?"

"Not right now."

"Ma, I don't know what to do," Robin said as he pulled the butter dish out of the fridge and a knife from the drawer. He leaned against the counter and waited for the muffin to toast. Finally it popped up, and he buttered both halves liberally. "I think he's in love with me, too."

"So other than the obvious, what's the problem?"

"He's not out."

"At work?"

"Everywhere. He's deep in the closet because of this contract he's got with the owner of the practice who just happens to be a major homophobe."

"Why are *you* working for him?" she asked, suddenly uncomfortable that he'd put himself in this position. Denise was nothing but practical, having seen the ugly side of life at an early age. She knew what kind of evil lurked out there, and the thought of her son being exposed to irrational hatred frightened her. "Does he know you're gay?"

"I never said a word, so, no, he doesn't."

"Good Lord! You live in San Francisco, Robin; surely you could have found a gay-friendly office?"

"Look, Ma. I'm a male hygienist in a female-dominated field. You have no idea how lucky I am to be working for this guy." Robin paced, holding the muffin in one hand and taking savage bites out of it. He continued, waving it around like a baton, "He has a kickass reputation and a huge, successful practice. Just having his name on my resume will look good."

"All right, already, I hear you. What about this Scott, though? Why is he working for someone like that if he's gay?"

"Same reason: the money, the career."

"Then you guys will just have to be careful. Don't act like lovebirds at work."

Robin rolled his eyes, "I never act like a fucking lovebird, Mother."

"Oh, don't 'mother' me!" She threw a pillow at him. "I'm sure you have your own version of being lovesick."

"That's another problem entirely," Robin stated, his facial expression turning serious.

"Get over here," she said, reaching forward and grabbing Robin's hand to pull him toward her. He plopped down on the sofa, laid his head on her lap, and stretched out, letting her play with his hair the way she always did whenever they had their heart-to-hearts.

"I don't want to pry, honey. You'll tell me when you're ready."

"I think of him day and night, Ma. It's driving me a little crazy."

She smiled down at him and said, "Sounds like you're definitely in love."

"I feel like I'm losing control of the situation."

"Why does it have to be a control thing, Robin? When two people are in love, it's about giving. Power and control are about taking, hon."

"But how do you turn over your life to a complete stranger just like that?"

"It's not about handing over a life, it's about sharing one; becoming equal partners."

"It's not that simple."

"It can be if you let it."

"If it's so simple, why'd you never get married?"

"My prince missed the bus."

"Come on, Ma. What's the real reason? You didn't want to give up control, did you?"

"No, that wasn't the case." Denise looked down at her son and frowned, thinking about how to answer his question. They'd always been honest with each other, but surprisingly this question had never come up until now. "I guess there was a part of me that didn't want to share you, to risk having a stranger come into my life and tell me how to raise you. I wasn't going to put up with that."

"See! It's all about being in charge of your life."

"It's different when a child is involved. I'd fought to have you, Robin, despite everyone's predictions that you would endanger my life. Then when the birth turned out better than anyone thought it would, the government agencies tried to convince me to give you up for adoption."

"Why?"

"They didn't think I'd want you."

"How could you not want me?" he asked, the grin extending into a smile that went from ear to ear.

She laughed and picked up his hand and kissed it. "You were the most precious baby, even if you did look like a little bird covered with downy, peach-colored fuzz."

"Hence the name."

"For Robin redbreast," she nodded, a little embarrassed by the admission.

"You're cute."

"We're digressing here."

"I know," Robin said, sitting up and grabbing the remote. "Let's not talk about this anymore. Would you cut my hair, please?"

Chapter 13

"IT'S just like old times, huh?" Susie asked, lifting the frozen margarita up to her lips for a sip. She was surprised to get Scott's call last night, since he'd made no attempt to socialize after she'd arrived in San Francisco. He'd kept their relationship very businesslike, strictly doctor/assistant, probably because they did share a past and now their dynamic had changed. The fact that she was aware he was a homosexual left him a little vulnerable in this new position, and he probably wanted to make sure that she kept her boundaries.

"Not quite," Scott replied with a slight grin. "I haven't been in a straight club in years."

"I know things are strange right now," she acknowledged, "but it'll get better once you're rid of Dr. Morris."

"It couldn't get here any faster, believe me. The man's a fanatic."

"He's a jerk," she added. "Furthermore, he sucks as a surgeon. Have you noticed that his head is up his ass half the time? If it weren't for Jenna, he'd be performing surgery on the wrong side of the mouth. Thank God he's not doing implants. You'd have a lawsuit every other day."

"He promised he would never attempt one, although he's starting to get more and more interested. He seems to think it's as simple as digging a hole in the ground and planting a tree."

"Shows you how much he knows… it's the money he's interested in, not the procedure."

"True."

"Has he said anything to you about the two of us?" Susie asked, curious to know if Dr. Morris had shared his thoughts.

"Uh huh… seems to think we're a match made in heaven."

"He's insane. Scotty, why are you with this guy? Surely you could have bought into another practice?"

"It fell into my lap, Suz. His lawyers actually sought me out after I won the AADR award. I was interested because of the location of his practice and the fact that he has a great reputation."

"But after your first interview, didn't you realize he was a spokesperson for Promise Keepers? That he was a fucking zealot when it came to gays and marriage?"

"I guess I chose to ignore it. You know how much I wanted to get away from my folks."

"I also know what you've sacrificed to be such a success."

"We've both had our fair share of drama, haven't we?"

"Yup… we haven't exactly lucked out when it comes to parents."

"At least you have a great mom, even though she's sick right now. She was a good mother when she was younger, and your stepfather dotes on you."

Susie laughed at that statement. "He bribes me, Scott. He couldn't care less about me as a person." Susie stood up wanting to drop the entire subject of parents. "I'm going to the restroom. Don't be picking up any hotties while I'm gone."

"Hardly," Scott mused. He ran his right hand through his hair and stared out at the crowd of dancing couples. He was hit by a sudden longing for Robin that left him practically in tears. He thought that being with Susie tonight would help, that being in a crowded space would take his mind off the redhead, but all it did was reinforce the fact that he missed him terribly. He missed his smile, along with the freckles and the strong hands running up and down his body. He kept seeing Robin's wicked grin as it appeared seconds after the wink which would send him to his office or the restroom and leave him in a state of high arousal. He moaned quietly when thinking of Robin jerking off in front of him, all the while searing him with the startling blue eyes that saw right through all his different layers. Robin knew what made him tick; every needy, submissive part of him had been offered to him without hesitation, yet it didn't seem to be enough.

A large part of Scott's disquiet had to do with the uncertainty of their arrangement. It's not like they were contracted in any way. Robin could walk out the door at any time; leave him to find another Dom and hygienist. He knew Robin was attracted to him, that he had feelings beyond their D/s relationship, and maybe that was what was freaking him out. He didn't seem at all comfortable in relinquishing his dominant role, a fact made painfully obvious the other night when he refused to be topped.

Scott could deal with that, though. He had no need to be dominant or top if it wasn't what Robin wanted, but he'd taken off before he could even tell him that. Scott had planned on talking to him tonight, to let him know that he was willing to become his contracted sub. But it appeared that he'd misread the whole thing. Robin didn't want to be in a relationship with him because he couldn't blend everything: Dom, lover, and employee, all-important facets of their budding relationship that were clashing right now, as incompatible as oil and water. Nothing and everything seemed to be working, and maybe that was the reason Robin pulled away suddenly.

He watched Susie walk across the dance floor, making her way back to their table. A guy in a red shirt, nice looking in a muted, respectable sort of way, stopped her. Not really her type because his hair was too short and his muscles not so pronounced, but she seemed pleased with the attention and was flirting right back. Scott thought back on all they times they'd gone out cruising only to part at the end of the night. Tonight was falling into the same pattern. He figured he'd be walking out of the club by himself.

"Scott, this is Jonathan," Susie gushed, introducing the two men.

"Nice to meet you," Scott said politely. "I'm planning on leaving soon. You ready to go?"

"You're not going yet, are you?" Jonathan asked Susie, hoping she'd stay.

"Not if you offer to drive me home."

"I'm offering."

"Do you mind?" she asked Scott, knowing he wouldn't mind at all.

"No, but I want to make sure you get home safe and sound. Can I see your driver's license?" Scott asked, surprising Jonathan with the request. He had no idea that Scott had a photographic memory, and by the time Scott handed back the card, he'd memorized his home address and license number.

Scott walked out of the club and drove home. He got to his apartment and started stripping as soon as he walked through the door. He left a trail of clothes and got into the shower, turning it on full blast, wishing that Robin was waiting for him in bed.

He soaped and rinsed off quickly, pulled a white towel off the heated rack, and padded back out to the kitchen where he saw his house phone was blinking. It was odd that whoever had called hadn't used his cell phone. It was with him at all times; he gave out that number to his patients. He hit the button and listened to the message.

Hey, it's me. I'm sorry I left in a rush... I don't have your other number keyed into my phone... um, don't ask me why I left 'cause I don't have the answer. Seems like I don't have the answer to a lot of questions right now... I just know one thing for sure... I miss you, baby... I miss you so much I hurt... call me?

Scott's jaw dropped, and he made a mad scramble for the employee phone directory, looking up Robin's cell number. He hadn't left it on the cryptic message, and when Scott finally found the list with all the phone numbers, he dialed, praying Robin would pick up even though it was almost two in the morning.

"You got my message," Robin sounded sleepy but happy to hear from him.

"I woke you?"

"It's okay. I wanted you to call."

"Red?"

"What, love?"

"Don't run from me." Scott's voice shook as all kinds of emotion raced through him.

"I'm sorry, baby."

"Can we please talk when you get back? I want you in my life."

"I'm not sure this is going to work."

"I know you have lots of questions, and so do I, but we need to communicate, don't you think?" Scott was desperate, practically holding his breath to hear Robin's answer.

"It would be a good start."

"How soon can you leave?"

Robin chuckled softly, "Do you know what time it is?"

"Yes. I don't care. I'll come and get you."

"Now?" Robin was surprised by the urgent tone.

"Please, I can be there in about an hour."

"Scott."

"No, no Scott tonight, just your love."

"My love," Robin responded gently, meaning every single word. "Why can't this wait until tomorrow?"

Scott's voice came out in a ragged whisper, "I need you, Red."

"Come and get me," Robin's reply was gruff, his senses filled with a powerful emotional rush as he listened to Scott beg. "Call me as soon as you hit San Ramon, and I'll give you directions."

"I'm walking out the door in five minutes."

"Love?"

"What?"

"What are you wearing?"

"Blue jeans and a T-shirt."

"Anything else?"

"Nothing."

"Hurry, baby…."

Chapter 14

THEY came together in a searing, open-mouthed kiss that left them both trembling with desire. Scott moaned as Robin tore at his T-shirt, lifting it off his body, running powerful hands across his flat, muscled torso, paying special attention to the hard nubs that puckered in response. "God, you are going to drive me insane," Robin moaned before he took one of the nipples in his mouth and flicked his tongue around it, followed by sharp nips of his teeth that made Scott cry out loudly.

"What do you want from me, love? Tell me what you want," Robin said, his words muffled as he continued to minister to Scott's nipples, now transferring his attention to the other one while his hands explored roughly. He cupped Scott's groin and squeezed at the erection that was clearly outlined against his pants. "You're beautiful, baby, so fucking beautiful." Robin's words came out in a soft, breathless whisper. "Always so ready for me."

He fumbled with the button of Scott's blue jeans, drunk with anticipation, knowing full well that Scott was going commando again. The zipper slid down easily, followed by his pants as Robin yanked them down around Scott's hips to free the engorged shaft that bobbed at him temptingly, beckoning him to wrap his lips around the smooth, taut skin that felt like the finest silk in his mouth. He could hear Scott moaning with pleasure as he slipped his swollen cock in and out of his mouth. Scott gyrated against him, lifting his hips to try and push his cock further down Robin's throat. "Red… yes… oh God… that feels so good." He clutched at Robin's hair, pulling at the strands while he moved Robin's head up and down, helping him along.

Robin inserted a finger into Scott's asshole, feeling his sphincter tight around it, and moved it slowly, searching for that one sweet spot that made Scott convulse when he finally found it. Robin heard Scott cry out, seconds before the hot streams of salty-sweet come rushed into his mouth and down his throat while Scott undulated and rutted against him. "God… I… love… you," Scott whispered, overcome with emotion. He lay boneless and pliable across the leather seats of his BMW that was parked in front of Denise Kennedy's apartment.

Robin's senses were on overload. Scott's words, his taste, and the pungent smell of two men in a state of high arousal goaded him into pushing his own pants out of the way and kicking them off his legs impatiently. His fingers shook as he rolled the lubricated condom on himself and turned Scott, lifting him on his hands and knees. He looked beautiful and sultry in the shadow of the street lamp, offering himself without hesitation as he spread his legs wider giving Robin the access he needed.

Robin buried his face against Scott's luscious cheeks, separating them with strong hands so he could lick at his entry, preparing him for the next few seconds. Scott's reaction to his ministrations set him on fire, the mewling sounds he was making as he lapped at the wrinkled skin drove Robin to the brink of a fast-approaching orgasm. Finally, when he could wait no longer, he plunged into Scott, sinking past the tight muscles, lifting his ass higher, allowing him to burrow in until his balls touched the warm skin and he heard the loud, harsh sounds coming from Scott's throat. Robin plunged repeatedly, grazing the gland that made Scott cry out with each thrust, and he squeezed his lover's hips with strong fingers, marking him with an imprint that would linger for days.

"That's it, love, move your beautiful ass… let me fuck you till you scream." Robin huffed against Scott's neck, each thrust of his pelvis pulling out a ragged groan from deep in his chest. "Say you're mine, baby," Robin urged.

"Yes, yes… oh fuck, yes, I'm yours, Red," Scott cried out eagerly as Robin never let up on his movements, reveling in Scott's pliant body. His cries and whispers, and every needy sound acted as the finest aphrodisiac pumping into Robin's blood stream, making him forget all his doubts.

"Hurt me," Scott exclaimed loudly, "mark me... Red... make me yours!" His voice broke, switching to deep moans that seemed to wrap themselves around Robin, adding to his pleasure as he plundered balls-deep with each thrust. Robin tried to slow things down, to draw out the sensations, but Scott's words ignited him, pushing him forward much too quickly. He moved his hand down and curled his fingers around Scott's thick and swollen cock, despite the earlier blowjob, adding more to the erotic mix that swirled around them, pushing him forward until he was minutes away from his own climax. He bit down on Scott's shoulder, and heard him scream, setting off the chain of events that finally pushed him over the edge as he came in endless spurts of hot semen that filled the head of the condom while Scott's seed spilled all over his hand in a warm, white gush as he milked him in time with his stuttering hips. "Scott... yes, all mine, baby... you're mine!"

He collapsed on Scott's back, struggling to get the air into lungs that were tight with emotion, and when he finally did, he let out a huge breath and lay lifeless, drained by the rush of adrenaline that saturated his body followed by the lethargy of sexual release that left him almost drugged with pleasure.

They dozed, each one sated and replete. About a half hour later, Robin woke to find himself still draped over Scott as they lay spread out on the back seat of the vehicle. He pulled away, his cock slipping out of Scott's ass easily, and he removed the condom and dropped it on the floor, making a mental note to get rid of it later.

"Scott, baby, wake up." He shook Scott gently, kissing him at the base of his neck, running his lips lightly around his ears and smiling when he heard his sub moaning with delight.

"Let's go upstairs and take a nap. We'll leave for the city when we wake up. "

"Okay," Scott replied, moving like a zombie, pulling his pants up and slipping on his T-shirt and shoes. Robin took Scott's hand and led him up upstairs into the apartment, and they curled up on the sofa, spooning against each other, asleep within minutes.

THE humming was the first thing that woke him; the smell of coffee and frying bacon was next. Scott worked his way out of Robin's embrace and opened his eyes to the sight of a middle-aged woman in light blue sweat pants and a pink T-shirt standing in front of the range, turning pieces of bacon in the frying pan. Her back was to him and all he could see was auburn hair caught in a low ponytail. He studied her silently, noticing she had a slight hump just off her right shoulder blade. She was slim, around five foot ten, with milky white skin on her arms, minus the freckles. She was humming and wiggling her hips, doing a cha-cha of sorts as Gloria Estefan and the Miami Sound Machine belted out their Latino rhythm from the small radio on the kitchen counter. She suddenly turned, sensing his eyes on her, and smiled warmly when she saw he was awake.

"Hello! You must be Scott."

"Good morning," Scott answered, running his hand through his hair, which felt knotted and tangled. He was embarrassed to be caught in the arms of her son in the middle of her living room. Thank God they had their clothes on, or he'd have died of shame. "Sorry about the sleepover."

"It's no problem at all," she answered warmly. "My name is Denise Kennedy. Would you like a cup of coffee?"

"I'd love some."

She poured some coffee into a white mug and walked over to hand it to him. Scott noticed the limp and the sideways pitch of her body but forgot it immediately when she smiled at him. She had one of the most beautiful smiles he'd ever seen. Radiant was the word that came to mind. Her eyes were grayish-blue and shaped like Robin's, but her palette was subdued, a far cry from the striking blue hues that Robin seemed to own.

"Is black okay, or would you like something in it?"

"Black is fine. Thank you."

"Mama," Robin mumbled from his position on the couch. His face was pressed to Scott's backside, and he slid his arm around Scott's waist as he held him tightly. "You two meet?" he said, stifling a yawn. He was emotionally exhausted and could have slept for another four hours; however, he knew they had to get going, so he forced himself into an upright position. He raked both hands through his wild mane and looked at Scott and grinned. "Morning, love," he said softly, bending forward to kiss him on the mouth.

Scott was taken aback at this display in front of Denise, but responded appropriately, saying good morning right back.

"So this is your Scott," Denise said, smiling at Robin.

"This is," Robin answered easily. "Isn't he beautiful?"

"Robin!" Scott said, the color rising to his cheeks quickly.

"It's okay, baby. She knows all about you."

"Don't be embarrassed, Scott. I'm delighted to meet the man who's been rocking Robin's world."

"I have?"

"You know you have," Robin said passionately, grabbing Scott's hand and pulling him close. "Sit right here, love."

Denise was delighted to see the look on Robin's face and the equally enamored gaze emanating from Scott's eyes. It was quite obvious that they shared something very special.

"Do you guys want breakfast? I'm frying some bacon right now. I can make eggs and toast to go with it."

"Sounds great, right, Scott?"

"Yes, it does. I need to use the bathroom," Scott stood, looking around the small apartment to see if he could spy the door.

"It's down the hallway to your left," Denise said. "There's a fresh towel in the cabinet under the sink. You're welcome to take a shower if you'd like."

"No thanks on the shower, but I'll use the towel for my face. I don't suppose you have a spare toothbrush?"

"Are you kidding? My kid is a hygienist. We buy them by the gross." Denise laughed gently.

"I know," Scott replied, "I'm just as bad. May I have one?"

"Of course, they're also under the sink."

"Okay," he answered, moving away from the pair and heading down the hallway. He finished his morning ritual, washing his face and brushing his teeth as he stared into the mirror, wondering what she thought of him. It was the first time in years that he'd been comfortable in the presence of a stranger who saw him for exactly what he was, a gay man in love with another man. Scott had been living a lie on and off for so many years that he'd forgotten what it was like to be comfortable showing his true feelings in front of others.

He opened the door and ran smack into Robin who caught him easily, wrapping strong arms around his torso. "You okay, love?"

"Your mother is great."

"She's special."

"I know. I think I like her almost as much as I like you."

"Like? That's not what you said this morning."

Scott felt the heat licking his cheeks and he looked down at his feet and stammered, "Love, I think I love her as much as I love you." He looked up at Robin anticipating a rejection, and he held his breath waiting for the words to come.

"I think she loves you too, baby, as much as her son does."

"Does he?" Scott asked, unable to keep the joy from showing on his face. His smile alone was worth Robin's admission.

"You bet he does," Robin whispered fiercely, grabbing Scott's head with two hands and planting a deep, gut-wrenching kiss on him.

They moaned into each other, only breaking apart when they heard Denise yell, "Breakfast is ready!"

Chapter 15

THERE was a comfortable silence as the car left San Ramon. Scott reached over, and Robin took his hand, intertwining their fingers and resting their joined hands on the console between them. It was several miles before Robin said, "We need to talk, baby."

"I know."

"I want you to sign with me."

Scott looked over at Robin quickly and said, "You want to formalize this?"

"Yes. I'd like to, for the sake of my sanity."

"You know I'm committed to you, Robin."

"That's not the point. I need guidelines and parameters, love."

"All right."

"What we're trying to do is difficult at best and impossible without strict rules. I need to separate our different roles or I'll have to walk out of your life."

"No!" Scott looked at Robin in a panic. "Please, Red, don't say that."

"Hey," Robin said gently, squeezing Scott's hand. "No need to freak… I'm right here, wanting this to work."

"Okay." Scott calmed down, but was clearly unhappy with where the conversation was heading. "I need to pull over somewhere so we can talk. Do you mind?"

"That's fine." Robin looked around and realized they were almost in Berkeley. "Do you want to stop here or keep going? We're almost home, love."

"I guess we can keep on going," Scott answered, frowning slightly. "What are you so worried about?"

"The fact that you're my employer is a huge concern, not to mention this ridiculous charade of pretending we're straight for Ron Morris's sake."

"It'll be over in six months, Red. That's not such a long time." They stalled at the tollway waiting in line before crossing the Oakland Bay Bridge into San Francisco. Scott turned toward Red and continued. "When my contract is over and he walks out the door, we can be ourselves again and shed the whole straight persona."

"You'd still be my boss."

"Yes, I will, but I'd also be your submissive and hopefully your lover and your friend, right?"

"Can all three mesh?"

"I want it to work, Red. You don't know how much," Scott said softly, unable to keep the tears from appearing suddenly.

"Hey, baby," Robin was shocked by this naked display of emotion, and he quickly wiped away a tear that started to roll down Scott's cheek. "I'm here talking to you. That should count for something."

"But that isn't going to be enough if you can't get our different roles settled in your head."

"Have you?" Robin asked, just as the car started to move.

"I think so."

They were silent once more as the car made its way across the bridge and into the city. Scott took the Van Ness exit and quickly crossed town toward Nob Hill and Jackson Street. He hit the remote when they got to his apartment building and inched the car into his private space before turning off the engine.

"Scott, look around you," Robin stated bluntly. "You hold all the cards. It's *your* practice, *your* apartment, I'm *your* employee. Everything is yours, love. I bring nothing to this table."

"No, that's not true!" The desperation was now clearly evident in Scott's voice. "You bring yourself, something I could never buy."

"And I intend to keep it that way."

"What do you mean?" Scott asked.

"I think that the first order of business is for you to sign on to be my contracted submissive for the next six months. We can reevaluate our contract after that."

"I'm more than willing to sign," Scott said, "but isn't it just symbolic since you and I aren't really into the club scene? Who will retain the contract?"

"It will end up with my mentor, who's a part of the scene in a big way. He'll hold the contract."

"I had no idea you kept in touch with anyone from that world."

"Just because I don't go to clubs doesn't mean I'm not involved. There's an entire network of people who know me and call me for private scenes."

"Oh. Have you done anything private since we've been together?" Scott asked, possessive suddenly, afraid to hear that Robin had been seeing others.

"Not since I moved to the city."

"I'm glad."

Robin noted the obvious relief on Scott's face and continued. "As part of our contract, we need to define our roles clearly. During the work week, we'll have no scenes at all. It's too difficult to have an intense scene with you and then show up at work the next day without having it carry over."

"What about the little things you make me do?"

"That's going to stop. While we're at work, it will be strictly business."

Scott nodded. "I can deal with that. When would we get together for our sessions?"

"The weekends are all mine, love. We'll take casual Fridays to an entirely new level."

Scott finally smiled, visions of Robin's wicked games rushing to his head, opening up the floodgates of his imagination. "I can't wait."

Robin grinned and continued with his proposal. "As soon as Friday rolls around, you're mine to do with as I will. That includes erotic foreplay at work, and when we walk out the door on Friday night, I will be your Master and you become my sub until Sunday night, when we separate again for the week. The entire weekend will be all about putting you through the paces and pushing your boundaries, so to speak."

"What exactly do you mean?"

"I've gone easy on you, Scott. Our scenes are not as intense as they can be. You need to serve and submit and part of learning your role is to set daily chores and schedules. We'll have a morning and an evening session, punishment for failure and rewards for success. All of that will be laid out in the contract."

"I'm already hard thinking about it."

"You're a pain slut, love. My responsive, beautiful slut boy," Robin growled, bending to Scott to capture his mouth in a burning kiss. He bit his lower lip gently and said, "I love the fact that you're willing to let me have my way with you."

"Yes," Scott whispered, overcome with his desire. "Take me upstairs and make me fly, Red."

"We're not done yet," Robin said, pushing away and trying to control the rising passion. His eyes smoldered with want as the blood in his groin pulsed. "We've taken care of one side of our relationship, now we need to address the other."

"Which one?" Scott asked, trying to get his mind back to negotiations when it had clearly flown up to the playroom where visions of floggers and handcuffs danced around in his attractive head.

"The love we seem to share for one another."

"Seem? There is no seem, Red. I love you, plain and simple."

"And I love you, but it's not so simple with me, is what I'm trying to say."

"Why is this so hard for you?"

"I've never been in love with a sub, let alone anyone else. You're a first for me."

"I'm honored."

"Don't be," Robin stated, "virgins are a bitch to deal with."

Scott chuckled softly, completely charmed by Robin's honesty. "Red, I'm crazy about you, and the fact that I'm your first love is a huge turn on for me; I'd do anything to keep the position of first and only love."

"Yes, I understand, but I need to be able to explore this side of our relationship without feeling like a complete bottom."

"Is that so bad?"

"To me it is. I've never bottomed for anyone, but with you I've been tempted, and it's freaking me out."

"God, I love you."

"Scott, please let me finish."

"Sorry."

"During the week when I'm not your Dom, I'd like to explore being your lover and your friend."

"I want that, too, but how when we have to be so careful?"

"We'd play it by ear, but it would be Scott and Robin, not Master and sub, okay?"

"Isn't being a Dom such a big part of you, though? You've just said you'd never bottom, Robin. That means you're not willing to let the Dom side of you disappear for a few hours each day."

"I didn't say I never would, did I? I just said I never had."

Scott nodded, encouraged by the response. "I see. Do we need some sort of signal to alert us to this side of our role-playing? I don't want to ever overstep my boundaries with you. How do I know which persona is in front of me?"

"I guess we could have some sort of outward sign."

"Such as?"

"Hell, I don't know," Robin wondered, raising his shoulders, and his eyebrows as well. "How about a pack of gum?"

"Gum? That's not very romantic, is it?"

"I can't imagine what Susie or Ron Morris would say if I showed up with roses and laid them on your desk."

"That might pose a problem."

"Indeed," Robin responded. "Gum is much less obtrusive."

"All right," Scott agreed. "If I see a pack of gum on my desk, it's because Robin wants to ask me out on a date."

"Or just spend the evening with you."

"That would be great," Scott said gently. "Are we done? I need to be with my Master right now."

"Do you agree to all my terms?"

"Yes, more than agree. I welcome every last one."

"Then let's go upstairs and celebrate. I'm sure we can find something to entertain us," Robin said with that look in his eye again, the one that said "you are so mine."

THE celebration consisted of a long caning session with Scott ending up in subspace. It was almost ten by the time it was all over, and they moved out of the playroom and into the master bedroom. Scott laid face down on the queen-size bed while Robin applied the Vitamin E lotion liberally on the red welts that crisscrossed Scott's back, ass, and thighs, the visible reminder of his submission.

"You're beautiful, baby. Does this feel good?"

"Yes," Scott mumbled, floating in his happy place.

"Let me hold you," Robin said in a voice gruff with emotion. He'd ended up with tears pouring down his face when Scott broke, completely moved by his trust and willingness to place his life in his hands. It was a thing of beauty to witness, and each time they achieved this unique moment, Robin's feelings for Scott were only reinforced; the connection between them so solid.

"You're such a love, I can't imagine not having you in my life."

"Thank you, Master."

"You're welcome, baby. I should really get going."

"No, stay with me tonight," Scott insisted, wrapping his arms around Robin's torso. He had his head resting on Robin's chest, the honey-colored strands of hair fanned out in stark relief against Robin's milky white skin.

"We'll be trashed on Mondays if I stay over on Sunday night."

"I don't care. It's so worth it."

"Okay, I'll sleep here tonight, but in the future, we should have our heavier scenes on Friday night or Saturday, that way we have all of Sunday to recuperate. I think it's best that we sleep alone on Sunday night so we move out of the Dom/sub mindset to get ready for the work week."

"Next Sunday, okay? Tonight I want you with me."

"Okay, love. Are you hungry?"

"Yes, but I'm too comfortable to move. I want you to keep holding me."

"I love you, Scott."

"I love you too. Don't ever leave me again."

"I didn't leave you, baby. I just needed a time-out to think about how we're going to survive this."

"We'll survive it, so long as we're together. Promise me you'll never walk away from me," Scott's leaf-green eyes were shining when they looked up at him.

"Have you been left before, love?" Robin asked gently, running a strong hand over Scott's thighs, kneading the skin.

"Abandonment is an issue I've dealt with for a long time."

"Who abandoned you, baby?" Robin's concern sprung forth quickly, his need to protect his sub paramount.

Scott huffed out a bitter laugh. "Oh, let's see. It started when I woke up in my first foster home."

"What?" Robin was shocked by Scott's statement, his vision of the perfect upbringing completely shattered. "I thought your parents were still alive and living in Michigan?"

"I'm adopted, Robin."

Chapter 16

IT was Wednesday, and Scott had just completed a two-hour procedure when he walked into his office and saw the pack of sugar-free gum on his desk.

His heart rate sped up, a common reaction to the thought of spending time alone with Robin. They hadn't been together since the weekend, and he was having serious withdrawals. He looked at the schedule and saw that a hygiene patient was just about due for his exam, so he got up to go and check on him.

He observed Robin from the doorway. The head of red curls bent over the patient while he spoke softly, moving his strong hands back and forth, finishing up the hour-long session with the usual flossing. Sensing a pair of eyes on him, Robin looked up and smiled, warming Scott with the sheer joy of his presence.

"How are we doing today?" Scott addressed Robin and the patient as well.

"There's some puffiness on eighteen, but other than that, Roger is doing great," Robin answered.

"Good to know," Scott replied, pulling on a pair of gloves. He took the seat that Robin vacated and proceeded with his exam. He finished up in a few minutes and spoke to Robin, "I think if you scale around this area, it should clear up quickly. Maybe some Arestin might be in order."

"Yes, Doctor."

"Robin will take care of that one trouble spot, Roger. He's going to anesthetize the area so he can get in a little deeper, and then he'll put an antibiotic powder into the pocket. It's usually very effective in reducing the swelling. I'll check you again in a week to see how you're doing."

"That sounds great, Doc."

"Okay, Roger. It was nice seeing you."

"You, too, Doc."

"Robin, when you dismiss Roger, I'd like to see you in my office."

"Yes, Doctor," Robin replied, flashing him the smile again.

Scott walked out of the room with a half-hard cock, imagining all the wicked things Robin would do to him tonight. He barely made it through the next hour without giving in and jerking off in the bathroom, but he held off, wanting to save himself for later.

There was a knock on the door, and Robin poked his head in. "You wanted to see me?"

Scott held up the pack of gum and asked, "What did you have in mind?"

"How does dinner and a movie sound?"

"Real good," Scott replied. He got up off his chair and walked to the door to be closer to Robin. "Meet me at the garage after work. I'm parked on the third floor, three-fourteen, in my usual spot."

"Okay."

"Robin?" Scott held his arm to prevent him from leaving.

"Yeah, baby?"

"I love you."

"Love you too, babe. I've got to run."

"Okay."

The rest of the day was uneventful, except for one dark moment when Ron Morris decided to observe an implant case. Scott was placing one implant in an upper anterior on a young man who'd gotten his tooth knocked out in an accident. He'd taken a bite out of the steering wheel of his car when he'd swerved to avoid hitting a pedestrian. He ended up hitting a telephone pole instead knocking his tooth out in the process.

"This will be just like your own tooth once we get done," Scott told the patient confidently. "You won't even know it's there."

The patient gave Scott the thumbs-up, and they began the surgery. Everything went smoothly with the Scott and Susie team working in perfect rhythm, passing the drills in sequence to prepare the site before the implant was placed. Ron observed the entire procedure, and Scott tried not to think about the reasons why Ron would be in there watching. He just stayed focused on his patient and hoped that Ron Morris was just passing the time and not actually contemplating a surgery on his own.

He was getting ready to leave for the day when Ron stopped by his office and sat down in the chair in front of his desk. "That implant case was very nice."

"It will be perfect once it's restored."

"Yes, it was very nice."

"Ron? You're not actually thinking of doing implants are you?"

"Why not? The money is too good to pass up."

"Because you'll be retiring in six months, and it takes special training, as you well know. You haven't taken a single course in placing implants."

"Why take a course when I can watch you?"

"Because you need hands-on experience, Ron. You know that for a fact."

"Don't you be worrying about me, Scott. I was doing periodontal surgery long before you were even born. I am more than capable."

"I don't doubt that, Ron. If you really want to do this, why don't you take a course? Most implant systems offer them sporadically. I'm sure we can line one up for you."

"I don't need one."

"I'd feel better if you took one."

"You're not the boss yet!"

"I'm aware of that, but I'm about to buy into this practice, and I'd rather not buy into any kind of problems that you may leave me."

"I've haven't had a problem in over thirty years. What makes you think I'm going to have one now?"

"I'd feel more confident if you just stayed away from implants in general."

"You worry too much, Scott."

"Ron."

Ron waved him away, shrugging off his concerns as if they meant nothing. "Have a nice evening, Scott."

"You too," he replied, annoyed that he hadn't gotten any kind of assurance that Ron would drop the entire notion of trying out the more complex procedures that involved dental implants.

He finished dressing into his street clothes, made his way out of the office and took the elevator to the lobby. He turned left when he walked out the massive front doors and headed down the street to the Sutter Street Parking Garage. He took the elevator to the third floor and found Robin already standing beside the BMW with his backpack in his right hand. "Hey, you," he said softly, smiling when he saw his lover.

Scott quickly unlocked the doors and when they were safely within the confines of the car, protected by the tinted windows, he reached over and kissed Robin, moaning into him as their arms wrapped around each other possessively. "I've missed you." Scott huffed, caught up in his lover's familiar taste and smell.

"I know. It's been hell these last two days," Robin acknowledged.

"I don't think I can sit through dinner when all I want to do is tear your clothes off."

"Let's do takeout and watch a DVD at my apartment instead."

"What about my place? Won't we be more comfortable?" Scott asked.

"No, tonight is date night, love, remember? My terms, my apartment."

"Whatever you want, Red."

"Let's get some Indian food. Do you like curries?" Robin asked.

"Of course, they're spicy, aren't they?"

"Hell, yeah. They've got spicy that will make your hair stand on end."

"Go for it."

They ended up stopping at Dosa Restaurant on Valencia, calling ahead to pick up their order of lentil chicken and paneer dosa. The dosa was the specialty of the house, their famous signature Indian-style crepe with different fillings and assorted dipping sauces. Tonight they ordered the dosa filled with spiced grilled farmer's cheese and mango chutney for dipping.

"The smell is driving me crazy," Robin said as they drove away from the restaurant. "I'm so hungry I could scream."

"Hang in there, Red. We're almost at your place." Scott found parking easily, and they locked the doors and made their way upstairs. "I really wish you'd move," Scott said as they traversed the hallways to Robin's one-bedroom apartment. The smell of cooking was ripe in the air, a combination of grease and seafood.

"Mrs. Castro must be frying her usual," Robin said with a grin as Scott scrunched up his nose and pinched it with two fingers. "Oh, stop being such a priss," Robin teased. "It's just a little fried fish of sorts."

"It's disgusting."

Robin chuckled as he unlocked the door to his apartment. He double-locked it, placed the bag of takeout on the table, and reached for Scott, holding him lightly at the back of his neck while he proceeded to devour him with his mouth. "I thought you said you were starving?" Scott asked in-between hot kisses.

"I can't eat with a raging boner. It's very distracting," Robin said, pulling off Scott's shirt and fumbling with his belt. "Would you get this fucking thing off before I break it?"

"My, aren't we impatient."

"My, aren't we fucking beautiful," Robin said with a growl, feasting his eyes on the impressive package Scott displayed, *sans* underwear as usual.

Scott's grin quickly changed to a low moaning as Robin sank to his knees in front of him and took him in his mouth. "Oh God, that feels so good," Scott cried out, assaulted by the hungry mouth that was now sucking on him aggressively.

"Mine, baby," Robin said, twirling his tongue in maddening circles around the fat, rosy head while gently pinching Scott's balls with one hand. He snaked the other around Scott's hip and kneaded the plump ass that was now quivering with his desire.

"I'm so close, Red."

"Come for me, love, right now," Robin cried, pulling away from Scott for just one second before engulfing him again with his hot mouth. He sucked hard, humming as Scott's cock hit the back of his throat over and over as he began to thrust gently. Robin swallowed with each thrust, moaning softly as he felt Scott's cock sliding in and out, felt him hanging on to his curls and pulling tightly, felt the movement of Scott's hips increase as the thrusting escalated until the stream of hot come poured down his throat while his lover cried out, "Fuck me, oh my God, Red, yes, yes…."

Robin reached for his own cock that now ached with need and he wrapped his hand around it, clenching tightly as he came in sputtering streams, shooting spunk all over the floor as Scott sagged against him.

"Oh baby," Robin exclaimed, collapsing to the floor and rolling onto his back as he laughed gently. Scott knelt down beside him and draped his body over Robin's, showering his face with kisses, "Have I cleared your mind of all distractions?"

Robin's eyes were closed, and he looked completely blissed out. "Love, you can distract me all you want. I'd rather have your cock in my mouth than food."

"You know there's nowhere I'd rather be."

"I know, baby." Robin opened his eyes, settling the deep blue orbs on Scott. "I love you a little more each day."

"Red," Scott moaned, covering his lover's mouth with a blistering kiss that had a world of feeling behind it.

Chapter 17

THE empty cartons of takeout were piled high on the table thanks to the combined efforts of two healthy men.

They reclined on Robin's bed which was set low to the ground on a wooden pedestal that he'd bought from Ikea. It was covered with colorful throw pillows that acted as a headboard of sorts. They were naked, having discarded their clothes after the meal, and they had a light blanket thrown over them as they lay in each other's arms watching *Latter Days* on DVD.

"Aaron's hot," Robin stated, rubbing his fingers lightly over Scott's nipples.

"Christian is hotter," Scott countered, picking up Robin's hand and sucking on his fingers, one by one.

"Stop doing that or we'll end up missing the good parts," Robin growled, his cock already responding to Scott's tongue.

"Can't help it, this movie is making me horny."

"Susie did say you were attracted to brunets like Christian. Is he making you hot, baby?" Robin pulled his hand away from Scott's mouth and went back to playing with Scott's nipples, watching as they puckered instantly. "My beautiful responsive lover," Robin whispered, alternately licking and pinching the pink nubs.

"Stop it, Red. You know I get crazy when you do that."

"Baby, you get crazy when I do anything to you."

"I know, let's watch the movie. They're about to kiss."

"Fuck the movie," Robin growled as he pushed closer. He wrapped his hand around both erections, feeling their pricks turn slick with pre-cum as he massaged slowly. "Look at me, baby," Robin said, "I want to see your face when you come in my hand."

Scott was caught by the power in Robin's voice, unable to turn or pull away even if he wanted to. He could feel his heart beating wildly against his chest as Robin tugged and squeezed; he felt the orgasm slowly gathering in his balls as they moved against each other. They came in a rush of heat, his cry muffled by Robin's mouth as he consumed him in a scorching kiss. He heard the deep moans coming from Robin's chest as they continued to rut against each other in a warm and sticky mess.

"You're going to have to rewind this," Robin said quietly, holding Scott in a tight embrace.

"I want to be right here beside you," Scott answered, fighting to keep his eyes open. He was transported into a dreamy state, held down by the languor that swept through him.

"I'm right here, baby."

"Love you, Red."

"Me too. Scott?"

"Hmm?"

"Tell me about your childhood."

"Why?"

"I want to know everything about you. You already know about me and my mom."

"Your mother is pretty awesome, isn't she?"

"You don't know the half of it."

Scott pushed away and fiddled with the throw pillows, positioning them against the wall so he could lean on them comfortably. He gathered Robin against his chest and pressed his lips down on the red curls he loved and said, "Tell me the other half I don't know."

"We were dirt poor and lived on government aid for years. I think she was raped by my father, but she'll never admit it."

"And yet she wanted you," Scott said wistfully, twirling a red lock around his finger.

"Desperately, from what I can gather," Robin responded. "She's fiercely protective of me, but she's always given me my freedom. It's an amazing feat to do that, don't you think?"

"Do you know how lucky you are?"

"I know, love. I've always thought that, even when we had close to nothing."

Robin began to caress Scott's arm, gently running his hand across the lightly muscled forearm, playing with the soft blond hair that carpeted his skin. "What about you, baby? Tell me about your childhood."

"I don't remember much before the first foster home. I was left on a doorstep when I was a few days old."

"Shit! Was it a house or a hospital?"

"No, it was a church in Raleigh, North Carolina. I was raised by Catholic nuns until I was about four years old, and then I was placed in a foster home."

"How did that go?"

"They were looking for cheap labor. I had chores from five in the morning until six at night. We lived out in the country."

"You were four-fucking-years old!"

"I know, but I could still pull weeds and gather eggs from the henhouse. It was very Oliver Twist," Scott said in a voice steeped in misery. Robin looked up at him and put his hands on his lips.

"Let's not talk about this anymore, baby. It's upsetting you."

"No, I want to," Scott replied, determined to get through it. "I want you to know where I'm coming from and then maybe you'll understand why I've put up with Ron's contract and this need for subterfuge."

"It doesn't matter why you're doing this."

"It's important to me, Red."

Scott's voice shook as he spoke, the effort to describe his past quite apparent as his lips trembled and his eyes sparkled, turning them a much deeper green. His need to tell all affected Robin much more than his words. He cupped Scott's face with both hands and kissed him deeply. "Baby, you tell me whatever you want. Just know that I'll love you regardless, okay?"

"Okay," Scott replied, calming down a little bit. He lay back down on the pillows and hugged Robin to his chest as he started to talk in a quiet voice. "You have this preconceived notion that I was born with a silver spoon in my mouth, but that's nowhere near the truth, Red."

"I was wrong."

"I clean up real good," Scott said sarcastically.

"Hey, none of that, okay?" Robin chided.

"Sorry, I stayed with these people till I was about six, and then one day a couple came in a nice blue car and took me away."

"Who were they?"

"The Gregorys from Ann Arbor, Michigan. We drove for two days straight. I was told they would be my new mommy and daddy."

"How did they find out about you?"

"I haven't the foggiest, Robin. I've tried to investigate the circumstances of my birth, but there are no records. Nothing, zero, nada! I have no idea who my real parents are, and the Gregorys only said it was a closed adoption and that I would never have access to anything."

"What are the Gregorys like?"

"Good, decent people. I've never wanted for anything."

"Well, thank God for small favors."

"Until I told them I was gay."

"Oh shit!"

"Yeah, oh shit is right," Scott spat out bitterly. "I knew I was gay when I was a teenager, but I was always fearful of how they'd react. I was convinced that they would regret adopting me if they found out. So I became the model child instead, never drawing outside the lines, always the perfect student."

"Wow! That must have been exhausting."

"It was, so when I finally got to college I decided to reveal my sexual orientation. I'd hoped that they'd be more tolerant, after all, I'd done everything to make them proud, but they went off like a rocket and threatened to pull all financial support if I didn't change my wicked ways."

"Are they Bible thumpers?"

"They're Catholic."

"Same difference," Robin threw out.

"I was at Northwestern at the time, taking all my general ed classes before going into dentistry. Susie and I had just met, and she was with me the day I got the letter from my father. She nursed me through the worst hangover of my life, which led us to become very close. She offered to be my beard the whole time I was in Chicago. My parents were delirious with joy the first time I introduced her to them."

"That explains her statement about going after the same guys."

Scott laughed. "Yeah, we'd walk into a bar together and invariably end up being attracted to the same Latino hunk."

"And you end up with a redhead who's as pale as a ghost."

"I love my redhead," Scott growled, bending down to kiss Robin's mouth.

"And he loves you as well," Robin said reassuringly. "Tell me why Susie is the way she is with guys."

"I think she's also got abandonment issues. Her dad walked out of their house when she was very young and never came back. As a result, her mother turned into a bitter woman and bad-mouthed him all the time. Her stepfather seems okay, but Susie's not close to him."

"So she has trust issues as well. That's why she leaves men before they can leave her?"

"I suppose. It such a cliché, but it's a reality for her. She goes through them ruthlessly, discarding them like garbage once she's had her fill."

"Shit!"

"I know. I've been trying to help her with that, but I've gotten nowhere. Anyway, she was really cool about the bullshit with my parents. She even went home with me on holidays to reinforce their belief in our relationship."

"Have you told them the truth yet?"

"After I graduated at the top of my class and won a very prestigious award in the dental world, they stopped talking about it."

"The standard, 'don't ask, won't tell' crap."

"Yup."

"Huh. No wonder you're so comfortable with lying to Ron."

"I'm not comfortable!" Scott's voice rose, clearly offended by the statement. "I'm not a pathological liar, Robin. I just go into self-preservation mode."

"Whoa, baby, hold on. I never suggested you were a liar."

"What did you mean by that statement?"

"I guess I meant that you are aware of the dangers and know how to protect yourself."

"I'm a survivor, Red, an overachiever, driven and obsessive about my career and succeeding, but I'm not a liar," Scott said quietly.

"And now I see why," Robin answered, satisfied that yet another piece of the Scott puzzle was found and put into the missing space. "You're lying because you have to. It's a normal thing in our world. A lot of gay men can't come out at work, so they lie or omit the truth."

"I hate it, but I learned long ago that I'd have to resort to lies if I wanted to succeed."

"Do you really think they would have cut you off?"

"I know they would have, without a doubt! And if they knew about the other side of me, the submissive pain slut, they'd have me committed." Scott raked his hair with his fingers while sitting cross-legged and hunched over a pillow, rocking gently, to comfort himself as he'd done for years.

"Baby, come here." Robin's voice was as gentle as a mother's caress, the soothing balm Scott needed to ground him before he started to spiral out of control, a common occurrence whenever he thought of his childhood. "Let me make this all better," Robin said softly. "I know we're not in scene, but I think you could use a good spanking."

Scott choked back a sob and looked at Robin with eyes glinting like bright emeralds. "Please," he whispered.

Robin hauled him across his lap and rubbed his ass with a warm hand before he started to whale on him forcefully, eliciting a yelp followed by a deep moaning as he slapped Scott repeatedly with an open hand. "You're mine, baby. Never forget it."

"Yours."

"I will always be here for you," Robin said, his right hand never letting up while he watched with pleasure as Scott's skin turned a deeper pink.

"I love you, Red." Scott started to hump him, his prick leaking drops of come onto Robin's lap, mingling with his own juices.

"I know you do, baby. I love you so much… do you feel my love?" Robin asked, slamming an open hand in the center of Scott's ass. "I will keep you safe, love."

"Master," Scott let out a muffled scream as he buried his face on the mattress and moved his hips spasmodically, bucking against Robin's lap and now engorged cock.

"I need to fuck you, baby. I want your hot skin against mine."

"Yes, please, Red… Master… help me."

Robin reached for one of the condoms from the pile beside the bed and rolled it on himself easily. Scott moved off him and got on his hands and knees, widening his stance, clenching and unclenching his asshole as it quivered in anticipation, the delicate pink skin enticing Robin to press his tongue in a flat, warm lick, causing Scott to buck against him.

"Easy, baby."

"Fill me, please," Scott begged, "make me yours."

"You're mine, love, always and forever mine," Robin cried out as he slammed into Scott, thrusting against him repeatedly, driving in further each time.

"Love you," Scott said, his voice sounding ragged.

Robin bent down and whispered in Scott's ear, "Let go of the pain, love. I will always be here."

"Thank you, thank you, Red. May I come?"

"Together, love," Robin said, seconds before he snaked his hand around Scott's hip and clutched him in a warm grip that sent them both over the edge.

Chapter 18

FRIDAY arrived much sooner than expected. Robin was finalizing the contract he was going to present to Scott when they got together that night. He sat on one of the stone benches in Union Square, getting some sun while sucking on a lollipop from See's Candies. He knew it was the worst thing in the world for his teeth, but he didn't have much candy growing up, so it was always a big temptation when he walked by a store to not run in and buy something. Today he'd given in and savored the buttery, rich taste of the caramel.

He felt a rustle of cloth beside him and looked up to see Susie holding an iced coffee from Starbucks. "Am I interrupting anything?"

"No, I'm all done," he replied, folding up the paper and putting it away in his backpack. "Sit. We have about ten more minutes."

"It's beautiful today, isn't it?" she said, leaning her head back on the bench to catch the rays on her face.

"Yes. The sun feels great."

"If I were home right now, I'd be wearing a woolen jacket and gloves."

"I don't know how people survive where you come from," Robin stated.

"A lot of people don't understand how Californians live with the constant threat of earthquakes, so I guess it's all relative," Susie commented.

"To each his own, hmm?"

"Yup. You busy tonight?"

"It's Friday. Of course I'm busy."

Susie sat up, took off her sunglasses and lifted her eyebrows, "That was quick."

"What?" Robin asked.

"You have a boyfriend already?"

"Who said I have a boyfriend?"

"Well, I assumed that's what you meant about being busy."

"Hon, just 'cause I'm seeing someone doesn't make him my boyfriend."

"What's his name?"

Robin felt the heat climbing up his neck, and he knew that he was blushing. It didn't help that Susie was grinning at him as if she already knew the answer. "None of your business."

"Hah! I knew it."

"What?"

"You and Scott have hooked up, haven't you?"

"Shut up!" Robin replied, bending to retrieve his backpack. He slung it over his shoulder and stood up to go. "Come on, woman. We're going to be late."

"I won't say a word," she continued to talk, even as they headed back to the office building. "You have no idea how good I am at keeping secrets."

Robin stopped and looked her in the eye. "He told me. Thank you for watching out for him."

"You really care for him, don't you?"

"Yes."

"Well, if it's any comfort, the love oozes out of his eyes whenever you're around. I've never seen him this happy."

"Really?" Robin's pleasure at her remark was pretty obvious as his eyes crinkled and his smile extended from ear to ear. Susie couldn't help but respond in the same manner.

"You two are like fucking teenagers. You'd have to be blind not to see the attraction."

"Well, hopefully Dr. Morris is blind as well as dumb."

Susie broke out into a high-pitched laugh. "I don't think you have to worry. It would never occur to him that you two are gay. He's so clueless."

"Hope you're right, hon. Now, tell me about this Jonathan person that you've just met. You like him?"

"All his body parts seem to be working."

"Susie, stop it! You're acting like a jaded sixty year old."

"I know. I wish I weren't like this. Jon is really a nice person. I could learn to like him, but I know myself. I'll start thinking of ten reasons why he won't do, and I'll move on."

"Sweetie," Robin held her and stopped their forward motion. "You've got to let the past go. There are good men out there."

"Are there? I guess I just haven't found the right one."

"And you never will until you change your mindset."

"You don't know me, Robin," Susie said, starting to get defensive.

"I know a little bit from what Scott's told me. I know you're kind and loyal and always there for your friends and family."

"What else has he told you?" she asked, annoyed that Scott seemed to have aired her dirty laundry with Robin.

"Not much else. Scott just said that you are very picky and having problems finding the right guy."

"Oh." She seemed relieved by his answer, comfortable that he didn't know about her childhood or anything else. "Why should I settle? I want my relationship to be perfect."

"Susie," Robin frowned quickly and said, "There's no such thing as perfect. You'll be constantly disappointed until you admit that."

"Let's drop it, okay?" Susie asked. They were in front of the elevators waiting to go upstairs. "I appreciate your concern, but you're not my shrink."

"And I wouldn't want to be," Robin replied with an eye roll. "That doesn't mean that I don't care."

"You're sweet, Robin."

"I'm here if you need me."

She looked dubious but was willing to give him the benefit of the doubt, so she smiled and said, "Thank you."

"YOU want something to drink?" Robin asked, pulling the paper out of his backpack. He and Scott sat in a booth at the Bistro, one of the three restaurants at the famous Cliff House, overlooking the San Francisco Bay and its surroundings. The view was spectacular, and it was far enough from Union Square and Ron Morris to afford them the privacy they needed.

"I'll have a beer," Scott replied.

Robin raised his hand to catch the waiter's eye and ordered two Coronas and a plate of nachos.

"What's this?" Scott asked, picking up the paper and glancing at the words.

"Our contract."

"Do you want to go over the salient points, or do you want me to read it right now?" Scott asked.

"You can read and sign it later. Right now, let's just go over the important parts."

"Okay," Scott said quietly, looking at Robin with complete trust. "You know I'll sign, no matter what's on this piece of paper."

"I know, love, but we need to be responsible about this. It has to be mutually agreeable or it won't work."

"All right."

"After work on Fridays and until I leave your apartment on Sunday night, you'll be my sub, and as such will do everything I ask. You will exist to serve me."

"Agreed."

"I want you to call me Master the entire time we're together. Any slip will result in a punishment of my choice. This may include sexual deprivation, mild bondage, or physical work, such as cleaning the bathroom or the kitchen. I expect you to cook all our meals, and if you don't know how, you'll learn. I also would like you to be willing to try some of the things you balked at initially, when we first hooked up."

"What are you talking about?"

"Bondage."

"No! I told you I was claustrophobic."

"You told me that you'd never met anyone that made you comfortable enough to try these things. I'd like to push you to your limit, Scott, teach you how to free yourself and soar."

Scott's eyes glittered as he stared at Robin, and he said, "Okay. I trust that you'll stop if I start to freak."

"You have the safe word to use. It's still blue, right?"

"Right."

"Would you be willing to do scenes outside of the home, at a club out of town for instance?"

"So long as I'm masked and can maintain my anonymity."

"I would never jeopardize your status at work, Scott."

"I know, but I did have to say it."

"When we're at the apartment, I expect you to be naked at all times," Robin continued. "You can only come with my express permission, and if I want you in a cock ring or a butt plug, you'll do it. You will only dress if and when I say so or if we go out and do a scene. Is that understood?"

"Yes," Scott's voice had lowered a few notches, the arousal in his eyes clearly apparent.

Robin reached under the table and felt Scott's erection pressing against his pants. He smiled, satisfied that his sub was enjoying their talk and not freaking out over all his requests. "You're hard, love."

"Master," Scott groaned, reaching out to touch Robin.

"Soon, baby," Robin pulled back, avoiding his touch. "Just a few more things," he said. "I'd like to see you with a piercing and maybe a tattoo."

"What?" Scott asked, starting to get alarmed. "What sort of piercing?"

"A nipple ring or maybe even a Prince Albert."

"Oh, my God," Scott groaned.

"Only when you're ready, love. You would look amazing with a nipple ring that I could tug at, and a PA would drive us both insane."

"Please… stop," Scott begged, clearly wanting to take this to the next level. "I'm hard as fuck."

"I know, baby. That's the whole point, isn't it? Pushing you?"

"Robin, I agree to everything. Can we please go now?"

"No. We need to talk about your expectations as well. What are you hoping to get out of this relationship?"

"Isn't that obvious?"

"I need to hear it."

"I want to serve you, and in return I expect you to protect and cherish me, to guide me through the paces with respect at all times. I need to know you will always be there for me."

"That's a given, Scott. You will become the most important thing in my life, and I will never lose sight of that. I will be your champion, your lover, your master, and your friend."

"How long is this contract, Red?"

"Six months. Just as long as your remaining contract with Ron. We can renegotiate if it works out for us."

"Okay. Is that it then? Can we go now?"

"We can go after we finish our nachos. And Scott?"

"Yes?"

"It's after five. You're on my clock now. Don't use my name."

Scott's breath caught in his throat as he listened to Robin's dominant voice. His excitement gripped him, and he could barely squeak out the words, but he did, whispering, "Yes, Master."

"Good boy," Robin replied, patting him on the cheek. "Shall we hurry and finish our food? I have this need to feel your hot mouth around my cock."

Scott groaned, picked up his beer, and downed it in one gulp.

Chapter 19

SUSIE'S heart thudded against her chest, matching the pulsing cock buried deep inside her. She felt Jonathan's hot breath against her ear as he lay panting on top of her, completely spent.

"You're going to kill me, girl."

"It wouldn't be the first time," she quipped, feeling him slip out as he rolled over. She felt empty again, bereft of all feeling, a common occurrence after any sexual encounter. The high of the orgasm was always followed by the low of the separation. It was almost as if the loss of contact signaled her body to shut down and stop feeling.

She wanted him to stay inside her forever, but she knew he was done for the night. They'd been going at it since they'd finished dinner several hours ago. He reached over to the nightstand and fumbled around looking for the pack of cigarettes, and when he found it, he pushed himself up to a sitting position and lit one, inhaling deeply and letting the smoke out slowly, watching Susie as she got up and made her way to the bathroom.

"I really wish you'd quit that," she said, scrunching up her nose and making a face. "You have no idea how disgusting it is kissing a smoker."

"It didn't seem to bother you earlier."

"Earlier is different. We were at a bar having drinks and everyone around us was smoking. Here in the apartment everything smells so fresh and clean until you light up. I don't like it."

"I'll be more than happy to quit if you give me a good enough reason."

Susie stopped at the entrance of the bathroom and turned to him. Her naked body glowed golden in the soft light, and she could see that spark in Jon's eyes, the interest that lingered despite the fact that he'd already had several orgasms. It was usually at this point that men stopped looking and were more interested in getting some sleep or even worse, turning on the TV set to watch the news or a rerun of some sporting event. Jonathan was actually interested in talking to her, maintaining some kind of connection, even though his body was done for the evening.

"And what exactly did you have in mind?" she asked, unable to prevent the smile from creeping up on her face. He really was an attractive man even though none of his features stood out in any way. He was a brunet with ordinary brown eyes, but he exuded a quiet confidence that appealed to her, and he did have a killer body that he hid underneath the boring suit he wore during the day. When he told her he was a stockbroker, she just about shit thinking that he couldn't get more boring; however, he'd surprised her. Underneath that mild exterior was a creative and intense lover, someone who seemed to be able to match her libido, a first in many ways. He was also nice, which made it even more surprising. Usually the good lovers were assholes, thinking they were doing you a favor. Jon wasn't like that at all.

"Be my girl, Suz. Stop doing the bar scene."

"What?" She was shocked that he'd even go there since this was only their fourth date. "Aren't you jumping the gun here?"

"It's never too soon when you've found the right one."

She laughed out loud and looked at him in disbelief. "Are you serious?"

"Of course, I am. Come over here," he said, hoping she'd give him no argument. Susie moved to the bed and stood about five feet from him. "I'm not going to bite you," he said softly, reaching for her hand and tugging gently. "Don't you know I'm falling for you in a big way?"

"This is crazy, Jon. We just met."

"So?"

"So, I don't do relationships. I'm not the marrying kind."

He laughed and shook his head, putting out his cigarette in the small ashtray she'd condescended to provide. "That's supposed to be my line."

"Well, it's mine. I'm not interested in marriage."

"Did I ask for that?"

"Not really," Susie realized, a little embarrassed that she'd pre-empted him. "But you want to be exclusive, right?"

"Yes. The other stuff can always come later when we're both ready."

She started to walk away, heading toward the bathroom, but he moved forward quickly and grabbed her hand before she made her escape, pulling her back to him. "Why don't you let me try and make you happy?"

"Happy and marriage is an oxymoron."

"Let's drop the entire marriage issue. How about just being happy with a guy that's starting to fall in love with you?"

"Jon." Susie smiled at his statement although the joy never reached her eyes. They reflected a sadness that dwelled deep inside of her. "I don't believe in love."

He pushed the silky curtain away from her face and asked, "Why not?"

"I've never seen it. My parents split up when I was barely a toddler, and my stepfather wasn't all the affectionate with my mom. They seem to tolerate each other," Susie continued, trying to get him to understand where she was coming from. "Happily ever after seems to be a Hallmark catch phrase but has nothing to do with reality."

"That doesn't mean it can't happen for you," he said gently, touched by the vulnerable child she'd let him have a glimpse of. "You ought to know that everyone has a different path in life. Why are you so convinced that yours will parallel your mother's?"

"I'm not sure, Jon, and this conversation is getting way too intense." Susie stood abruptly and headed toward the bathroom, relieved that her back was turned so he wouldn't see the tears threatening to spill over.

"MASTER," Scott moaned, as Robin pressed the ice against his left nipple, causing Scott to twist around on the bed, trying to break free of the cuffs that had him tethered to all four posts.

They'd been at this for over an hour, and the torture with the ice had reached unbearable proportions as Scott's erection ached to free itself from the tight confines of the leather cock ring Robin had placed earlier.

"Please, let me come."

"Not until we're done with the piercing," Robin answered, reaching for the small case he had prepared with the sterile needle and alcohol swab. He pulled out the needle and rubbed the ice against Scott's left nipple again, making sure it was reasonably numb. "You ready, baby?"

"Yes." Scott's reply was breathless, and he stilled himself in anticipation of the pinch. Robin was straddling him, and he moved around trying to settle himself so that he could do this right. He'd pierced many nipples in the last few years, but tonight was different somehow. He wanted it to be perfect, because it was for Scott, his lover as well as his contracted sub. He positioned the needle and bent forward, and as he pushed into the tender skin, he lowered his face and covered Scott's mouth with his, relishing the sweet whimpers that came from Scott's throat, even as the needle went right through the skin. He broke away from the kiss and looked at his handiwork, satisfied that it was positioned correctly. The small gold ring he pulled out from the box had been lovingly purchased with his last paycheck, and his cock ached with need by the time he'd affixed it on Scott.

"Master," Scott begged, his eyes wild with anticipation, "please."

Robin released the cock ring and took Scott in his mouth. It was mere seconds before he felt the heat filling his mouth with a taste that was uniquely Scott's, the warm spunk coming in endless waves, accompanied by the soft moaning that drove Robin completely insane.

"Love you, Master," Scott sobbed, overcome by the intensity of the last hour.

"Love you, too, baby," Robin replied, pulling away and unhooking the leather cuff that tied Scott to the bed. His need was powerful, the pain in his balls and cock taking on astronomical proportions with each minute he had to wait. He could barely get the condom on, slathering the lube with shaky hands and finally, rolling Scott over and pushing into him, relishing the hiss that came out of Scott's mouth as he breached the tight entrance. "Baby," he groaned, "so good."

"Master...."

THEY must have fallen asleep because the sun had set and the apartment was cool by the time Robin opened his eyes and realized he was still on top of Scott. He fumbled for the condom that had slipped off his softened cock sometime while they slept. Scott was snoring softly; exhausted from the emotional roller coaster they'd ridden all afternoon. The nipple ring was the highlight of the scene, but the ice play had driven them both a little crazy. Who knew that such a simple tool could be so wicked?

Scott's face was turned to one side and covered by the luxuriant hair that gleamed in the reflection of the moonlight as it spilled into the room. Robin's heart rate sped up; overwhelmed by the sudden rush of love.

He walked over to the bathroom and stepped into the shower stall, rinsing himself quickly. The gray towel was warm when he pulled it off the heated rack and wrapped it around his waist. So was the washcloth that he grabbed and rinsed with warm water so that he could clean up Scott.

He perched on the side of the bed and shook his lover gently, bending down and moving his hair so he could kiss him on the cheek. "Wake up, love."

"Why?" Scott asked, turning and stretching at the same time, looking very much like a big cat.

Robin looked at the nipple ring, checking for redness or any sign of infection, and was relieved when nothing seemed out of the ordinary. He wiped off Scott's groin with the damp towel, gently lifting his cock and cleaning around his balls.

"That feels so good," Scott sighed, enjoying every minute of the attention that Robin lavished upon him.

"I can tell." Robin grinned as Scott lengthened and grew plump in his hand.

Scott opened his eyes and smiled at his Dom, pulling him close and kissing him on the mouth. "Thank you."

"You're welcome. Now get your ass out of bed and make me dinner."

"What? I have no fucking clue how to cook."

"Improvise."

"Improvise? How?"

"I don't know, but whatever you do, don't put any clothes on."

"Yes, Master," Scott replied, shaking his head and moving to the kitchen, trying to figure out what to make.

He ended up cooking scrambled eggs with SPAM and toast with butter and strawberry jelly, and served it with freshly squeezed orange juice.

Robin sat down and stared at the plate in shock. "SPAM?"

"Your point is?" Scott asked, raising eyebrows.

"Rich people don't eat SPAM," Robin said, questioning Scott. "Just us trailer trash."

"Well, I happen to like it," Scott said, "so that must make me trailer trash as well."

"I knew there was a reason I loved you besides your remarkable cock and deviant mind." Robin winked and attacked the food with relish.

"Don't get too excited about my culinary skills, Master. I can make breakfast, but not much else."

"You'll learn, love, and besides, I have breakfast for dinner all the time."

"Do you want me to kneel at your side while you eat?"

"No, baby. Sit at the table with me."

"Okay. Do you remember that we're going to Ron's house tomorrow?"

"Fuck, no! What time does he want us there and who's going?"

"He said around three, and I think the entire office will be there, along with his kids, their families, and his grandchildren."

"What's the occasion?" Robin asked, now munching on his toast.

"Wedding anniversary or some shit like that."

"Well, at least you won't have to cook tomorrow." Robin smiled.

"I'd much rather struggle with a meal than spend my Sunday with him."

"It'll be fine, baby. We'll still have the morning to play," Robin said, reaching across the table and flicking the nipple ring with his nail. His smile was genuinely depraved when he heard Scott's quick intake of breath. "Wait till you're healed, love. I'll drive you crazy with that," Robin said, practically burning a hole through Scott with his heated stare. "On your knees, love."

"Yes, Master," Scott answered, getting up immediately and sinking to his knees in front of Robin's splayed legs.

Chapter 20

"HAVE another beer," Ron said, passing the bottle of Corona to Scott. "Have you seen Susie?"

"She's over by the barbeque."

"I'm glad you came with her, Scott. You're finally starting to come to your senses."

Scott looked at his boss and wondered what drug he'd just ingested. "We didn't come together, Ron. We just got to the door at the same time."

"But now that you're here, you may as well leave together. Take her dancing or something."

"Give it a rest, will you?" Scott reached for the bottle of Corona on the table in front of him, stretching chest muscles that reminded him that he had a brand new nipple ring. He felt the heat course through his body, the sting around his nipple an instant reminder of his Dom and all they'd shared this past weekend. He looked around and spotted Robin chatting with Susie, and almost as if Robin could sense his need, he turned toward him and winked, settling that mischievous smile on him, the one that always got him straight in the gut. Scott smiled back then turned to Ron and said, "I've told you repeatedly that Susie and I are just friends."

"That can always change, my man." Ron stood and made his way over to Susie and the food station where his wife and daughter were preparing all the side dishes and the condiments. The actual grilling was attended to by Ron's son-in-law. Susie and Robin chatted while they waited for their burgers to cook as Ron came up to them and put his arm around her shoulder pulling her tightly against him. "How's my favorite assistant doing?"

"I'm fine, Dr. Morris."

"That's good." He turned his attention to Robin and asked, "How about you, Robin? Enjoying yourself?"

"Yes, thanks."

"Good. Eat as much as you like; we've got enough food for an army, right, sweetheart?"

Julie nodded an assent, smiling back dutifully. She was in her late forties, easily fifteen years younger than Ron and still a beautiful woman, even if a little worn around the edges from the many hours spent in the sun. She'd hoped to have a child, but it never happened, so she immersed herself in tennis, her friends, and her two standard poodles, who had become the children she never had. It was just as well, because Ron's son and daughter resented everything about her, and a new baby would have put the nails in her coffin in terms of any sort of relationship between them. The fact that she'd remained childless helped in their acceptance of her usurping their mother's place by Ron's side.

Ron's guilty conscience plagued him when it came to his ex-wife. She'd been his high school sweetheart, the mother of his two children, and he'd dumped her for the chance of getting Julie into his bed. He'd always been an attractive man and had strayed a few times in his marriage, but had never considered leaving his family until Julie came along. He'd stopped thinking with his head as soon as the cool brunette stepped into his office carrying a briefcase full of drug samples. The resulting scandal turned him into a guilt-ridden man who supported his ex-wife in the manner that would have been more fitting for a current wife. Annie Morris had never remarried, a situation that always bothered Ron and only increased his guilt. As a result, she still lived in their old home and continued to enjoy all the privileges of being a doctor's wife, better off financially than Julie would ever be. Ron preferred that Julie do without the new dress or a new car so that his ex-wife and children never wanted for anything.

Money was a bone of contention, driving a wedge between Julie and Ron as he continued to lavish his first family with whatever they wanted. His pursuit of Scott as a potential buyer was stoked by this need to settle his financial future as his retirement loomed ahead. Ron found himself in the incongruous position of a much younger man, hardly able to afford a lifestyle he'd become accustomed to because of all his financial obligations. As his sixty-fifth birthday and his impending retirement approached, he was faced with the sad realization that he wouldn't have enough money if he didn't sell his practice and make a deal that would allow him to continue collecting revenue from Scott for at least another year after his name came off the door.

Making sure Scott could come up with the money to buy the practice had become his new goal, and Susie was the meal ticket he needed to ensure that this would happen. He had no doubt that Scott could qualify for a bank loan, but why jump through hoops when he had a ready-made banker working by his side on a daily basis? He would not only solve the money problem, he'd be doing both Susie and Scott a favor. They were perfect for each other, and it was high time they settled down. It was starting to bother him that Scott didn't see it this way. Neither he nor Susie seemed at all interested in the idea of a union of any sort. Ron just couldn't understand why a young man in his early thirties had no interest in starting a family.

"Why don't we sit at a table once you've got your food together?" Ron said, signaling Scott to come over and join them. The entire party moved to the long picnic table set up on one side of the garden. Jenna had finally shown up with her friend, Gloria, the office receptionist of four years. They were both dressed in jeans and T-shirts, a fact that hadn't escaped Ron Morris. He frowned in disapproval, preferring that women dress in more flattering female attire such as dresses or if they must, pant suits, not jeans.

The meal proceeded without mishap until Ron's daughter, Victoria, announced that she would be joining the anti-gay marriage rally being held next week. She and her friends were great proponents of anything having to do with quashing gay rights. It had become her personal goal to see that Proposition 8 would never pass legislature, a goal Ron Morris fully supported. The apple obviously did not fall far from the proverbial tree, and homophobia flourished in Victoria's home, much to her father's delight. In fact, both his son and son-in-law were members of Promise Keepers, firm believers in the sanctity of the traditional marriage between man and woman.

"I'd like to propose a toast," Ron said, standing and holding a glass of white wine. "To my wife, Julie, who is like fine wine; smooth as silk and aging beautifully. Thank you for making the last ten years so special."

"Thank you, sweetheart. You don't look so bad yourself." Julie giggled, a little woozy from her fourth drink. "And here's a toast to all the single people at this table," Ron said, looking at Scott pointedly. "May you come to your senses and marry soon! There is a season for everything, and your time is now. Start your families; enjoy all the blessings that God will pour on you by being his loyal servants. Go forth and procreate!"

"So, if we're not married, we'll burn in hell?" Robin asked, unable to keep his mouth shut. He was flabbergasted by Ron's bullshit rhetoric and couldn't control the urge to put him in his place. "That whole business of procreation only made sense when the world was young, and there was enough food and space for everyone. We're living in a world that abounds with hunger and homeless people. I don't think it pertains to this century, Dr. Morris," Robin said bitingly.

"God's rules have not changed, Robin," Ron answered, fixing him with a glare.

"And that's where your religion is completely out of touch, Dr. Morris. It has not kept up with the pace of the modern world. People don't need to be married to have children anymore, if that's your big concern. There are hundreds of children out there who need families to adopt them, to give them a home because the good, God-fearing men and women who created them in a moment of passion have abandoned them."

"Those children are unfortunate, but not the rule of thumb. God intended for men and women to be together, to have families in the sanctity of marriage. He did not make us in his image so that men would lie with men or even worse, women with women. It's not God's wish that society denigrate the family unit that way. It's wrong, Robin."

"Daddy's right, Robin," Victoria interjected. "This is why we are joining together next week to protest the ridiculous voice of gay America that has arisen so blatantly, expecting all the privileges of normal people when clearly they are not normal."

"So, you're saying that all the gay men and women around the world are abnormal?" Robin asked incredulously. He couldn't believe what he was hearing.

"Let's just say that they need to be enlightened, and that's what we're here to do."

"You and your bible-thumping friends," Robin stated.

"Yes," Victoria replied coldly. "Are you gay, Robin?"

There was a huge crash as Scott tipped over two wine bottles, engulfing the table in a rush of red liquid that had everyone hopping around for paper towels. By the time they'd gotten the mess cleaned up, tempers had cooled and Susie had grabbed Robin's hand and steered him toward the house and away from the penetrating questions. Scott remained outdoors with the Morris family hoping to do some damage control.

"Well, I never expected that kind of attitude from one of my employees," Ron blustered. "Surely he wasn't serious."

"Robin was raised by a single mother," Scott said, hoping this would satisfy Ron.

"I see." Ron nodded, sipping from a fresh glass of wine. "No wonder he was a little defensive."

"Let's drop this entire line of conversation, shall we? We're here to celebrate, not have arguments," Scott asked. The last thing he wanted was for Ron to fire Robin.

"I'll drop it if you promise me that you'll take Susie home tonight, maybe stop and have a drink."

"That's fine," Scott said, having no intention of doing either.

"Good. You need to think about tomorrow, Scott. Living day to day isn't a good thing."

"I thought we were dropping this conversation?"

"Right," Ron replied, moving away from Scott and heading toward his family.

Scott took a deep breath, relieved that disaster had been averted, at least for the time being. He knew that eventually something like this would crop up again, and he prayed that he could convince his outspoken lover and Dom to cool it for another six months until Ron Morris no longer ruled their lives.

Chapter 21

IT was Monday night, a date night for Robin and Scott. The Dom/sub relationship was put aside for another week, tucked away in the closet along with all the paraphernalia that accompanied that lifestyle. The weekend had flown by, their spirits dampened by the incident at the barbeque yesterday.

They were on their way to south San Francisco to watch the movie *Unfaithful*. After last night's close call, they'd elected to travel the extra miles to avoid bumping into Ron Morris or anyone else they might know in the city. Someone had mentioned the booty shots in this movie, and they'd decided to check it out.

"You know, we could have just rented porn and stayed home," Scott declared.

"What fun is that? Seeing Olivier Martinez's naked ass on a big screen is much better. Besides, this way I can give you a hand job and watch you squirm."

"You wouldn't!"

"You don't think I will?" Robin grinned at the look of horror on his lover's face. Scott was so straight sometimes, Robin delighted in pushing him beyond his boundaries. "Come to think of it, we haven't done any real scenes. We need to plan something."

Scott took his eye off the road for a minute and looked at Robin with interest. "What did you have in mind?"

"Whatever turns you on, my love. Do you have a recurring fantasy? Some forbidden scenario you think about when you jack off?"

Scott laughed and said, "I have several, but there is one that keeps repeating."

"What is it?" Robin asked, excited by the prospect of learning more about Scott.

"Whenever we're at work and I walk by your room, I think about fucking in the dental chair."

Robin grinned at his lover. "Are you tied up?"

"I could be."

"My fantasy involves the same dental chair, but I see you trussed up with a pretty red rope against your golden skin."

"Oh my God," Scott groaned.

"Would you be willing to let me tie you down and put a gag on you?"

"I could go for the rope, but not the gag," Scott replied, a little breathless from the thought. He was completely caught up in the fantasy and the possibility of being dominated and bound was exciting him more than he thought it would.

"What about a blindfold?" Robin asked.

"That would work." Scott squirmed in his seat, uncomfortable in pants that had suddenly become too tight.

"Let's do it."

"How?"

"We'll go to the office next Sunday," Robin suggested. "We can play, and no one will be the wiser."

"I don't know," Scott voiced his misgivings. "It's sort of risky, don't you think?"

Robin leaned over and kissed him on the neck. "That's what makes it even hotter, love."

"Robin—"

"The thought of you naked and tied up is making me crazy. I can't wait to fuck you that way."

"Oh, God…"

Robin's hand found its way to Scott's groin, and he pressed the bulge, adding another dimension to Scott's misery. "This will give you something to look forward to all week, baby."

"What about now, Red?"

"You're a greedy man, you know that?"

"I guess I am," Scott could barely get the words out as his desire ratcheted up with the proximity of Robin's face and the busy hand at his burgeoning cock. "Can we go somewhere before the movie?"

"No, love."

"Please?"

"I'll take care of you in the theater."

"I don't want to get arrested for indecent exposure," Scott raised his voice in alarm.

"Baby, you've got to relax."

Scott continued to protest. "But—"

"Shhh." Robin covered Scott's mouth with his hand. "I would never put you in that kind of position."

Scott shook his head, imagining his picture splashed across the papers á la Pee Wee Herman. He could just see the headlines, *Prominent San Francisco dentist caught having gay sex in a movie house*. Ron would implode and fire him on the spot! He reached over to Robin and clutched his hand. "Let's just wait 'til we get home, okay? Please?"

"Okay, love." Robin didn't press the issue because Scott was about to have an anxiety attack, but he planned to revisit that one day. There was nothing more erotic than sex in forbidden places, and he wanted to show his straight-laced lover how good it could be.

Scott had seemed pretty uptight since yesterday's scene at the Morris home. It took hours for him to calm down despite Robin's assurance that he would do his best to avoid any more incidents with Ron. Even though Robin understood where Scott was coming from, he resented the fact that they had to live a lie for the sake of a man who treated him with contempt. The more he saw of Ron, the less he liked.

He was appalled that people like Ron Morris even existed. He'd never been subjected to this kind of mindset before, and he felt unclean just being around him. He was seriously contemplating looking for another job until Scott begged him to reconsider. "It's only for three more months, Red. Surely you can deal with it until then."

"I'm not sure that I want to subject myself to his brand of normalcy. People like Ron are ruthless in their beliefs, and he wouldn't think twice about hurting us if he were to discover the truth."

"I honestly don't see how he'd find out unless we did something really stupid. He's oblivious, can't you see that? His fucking daughter has better gaydar than he ever will, and she's only met you once. Ron has known me for almost nine months now and suspects nothing!"

"And they say that we're abnormal." Robin snorted.

"Hey," Scott continued to cajole, pulling Robin to him and littering kisses all over his face. "I love you so much… please don't even talk about finding another job. It would kill me if you left."

"I'm staying because of you. The money isn't important anymore. I've actually been able to save a little since I started, so I'd have enough to pay my rent while I'm looking for something else."

"No. I don't want you looking for another job!" Scott was emphatic but unable to disguise the almost desperate look in his eyes.

"Okay, okay. I promise."

After that promise, Scott was much calmer until this new discussion in the car. He seemed to have a real problem with the thought of jeopardizing his arrangement with Ron. Robin held Scott's hand until they got to the movie theater and only separated from him while they stood in the lobby to pay. Once they were in the darkened theater, Scott allowed Robin to slip his arm around his shoulder and leaned into him comfortably as they watched.

On the way home, Robin broached the subject of Ron Morris again, trying to understand why Scott felt Ron was his only option to making it in the world of dentistry. Scott was brilliant at his job and had excellent credentials. There was no reason why he'd have a problem finding another practice. Why insist on this one?

"Love?"

"Hmm?"

"Would you ever consider leaving San Francisco if this thing with Ron fell apart?"

"I like living here, don't you?"

"It's fine, but there are other places that are just as nice."

"Such as?"

"The East Bay? San Ramon is a nice town."

Scott smiled, recalling their meeting at the bar in San Ramon. "Who knew that one hookup would lead to this, huh?"

"Do you believe in fate?"

"Why?"

"My mother seems to think that fate plays a big part in what happens in our lives. I'm not so sure that's true."

"If it were true, there wouldn't be any point in trying to change things or make things better, would there? I mean if your life is already preordained."

"I think she meant more on a personal level, with people, you know? She feels that you and I were meant to be together. That it was in the stars," Robin said, recalling a conversation he had with Denise.

"The odds of our ending up together after that chance meeting were pretty poor, so I can go for her theory," Scott said, looking over at Robin. "I can't imagine how else we'd end up in the same city, much less the same office."

"It's good between us, isn't it?" Robin asked.

"Yes."

"Then what are you so scared of, love? Is the money all that important to you?"

"No," Scott said vehemently. "That's not it at all."

"Then what is it? Why subject yourself to this kind of bullshit when you could live a completely open life and be who you want to be."

"It's so easy for you to say that, Red. You know who you are, who your mother is. You're comfortable in your skin."

"And you're not? Will money and prestige give you the courage to be who you want to be?"

"Not the courage, but maybe the freedom."

"You're tying one with the other. It's crap!"

"You don't know everything, Robin. Don't tell me its crap!"

They'd arrived back in the city and were parked in front of Robin's apartment. Scott had turned off the engine, but neither man seemed to want to leave the car, preferring to finish their discussion right there and then. "Look," Robin said, unfastening the seat belt and turning to Scott, "at some point you're going to have to get past your issues of trying to be the best so that everyone will love you." Robin immediately regretted his words when he saw the hurt in Scott's eyes.

"Is that how you see me? Like some fucking insecure baby looking for love?"

Robin had been with Scott long enough to know when he was hurt, despite the bravura of his words. It killed him to see his lover this way, but this was a conversation that was a long time coming. "Isn't it true though? Haven't you spent your entire life trying to be perfect so that your adoptive parents would never regret taking you in? So that whoever abandoned you would be sorry they did?"

"What's wrong with wanting to be the best?" Scott said, trying desperately to keep the neediness out of his voice.

"Nothing, if you're doing it for the right reasons. It's wrong if you're using it as a crutch."

"There's obviously something wrong with me, Red. I mean, the whole submissive thing alone can't be normal."

"Normal? Is this really you talking, or are you buying into the Ron Morris school of stupidity?"

"What kind of normal person would enjoy being hurt? I've spent years trying to repress my cravings, but I can't seem to let them go."

"You are what you are, Scott. You enjoy being dominated as much as I love dominating you. There is no normal or abnormal in pleasure." Robin spoke gently, trying to help Scott sort through all his fears, but was clearly taken aback by the turn of the conversation. He had no idea that Scott still had doubts about being a submissive. He'd thought that it was the part of their relationship where he was most comfortable. "Baby, there's nothing more beautiful than a man who knows what he wants and is confident doing whatever it takes to achieve it. You are the perfect submissive, just as I'm a natural Dom. It's who we are, and I, for one, do not consider myself abnormal."

"I wish I could be like you," Scott whispered, looking down at his lap, trying to control his feelings and not think about the disappointment in Robin's eyes. "You had so little growing up, yet you're the most secure person I know."

"Baby," Robin said, lifting Scott's chin and seeing pure anguish. He reached for Scott and took him in his arms, kissing each eyelid, not at all surprised when he tasted the salty, wet eyelashes that betrayed

Scott's emotions. "I love you so much," he whispered reassuringly. "There's not one side of you that isn't perfect."

"What about all my hang-ups?" Scott asked, pulling back to stare into Robin's eyes.

"I wouldn't be with you if there was no kink. That's one side of you that I find particularly appealing. I also love the professional. Your competence during a surgical procedure takes my breath away. It's something you do effortlessly."

"Really?"

"Scott… don't you know how much I respect you?"

"I feel like such a fraud sometimes," Scott said. "I look in the mirror and see that kid that no one wanted."

Robin silenced him with a scorching kiss. He nibbled and licked, sweeping his mouth with an aggressive tongue, losing himself in Scott's unique taste. This was the man who had become his world in such a short time. This complex individual who was so much more than the perfect package he presented to the world. Loving him came as naturally as breathing, yet Scott was plagued by irrational fears that could easily take over if he allowed them. Robin was determined to wipe those fears away, to help Scott overcome the need to prove something to the phantoms of his childhood and the specters that haunted him now, making him feel less worthy than anyone around him, despite the obvious success he'd achieved in almost anything he touched.

"Scott, let's go upstairs."

"Do you still want me after all the crap you've just heard?"

"I'll always want you, love."

Chapter 22

THE apartment building smelled of fried fish again, but Scott only smelled Robin.

He was captured by his lover's musky scent, the taste of his skin, the look and feel of his hair as the tight coils caught in his fisted hands. "I love you," he growled, feasting on the mouth that had managed to assuage his fears for one more night, to reassure him that he was worthy of love.

"Baby." Robin's sighs of contentment were the only signal Scott needed to proceed with his assault.

He poured out his love in burning kisses that scorched Robin, igniting every inch of his muscular body with desire. He attacked the dark nipples that puckered in anticipation, sucking hard, drawing out moans that sent signals straight to his tumescent cock.

"That's it, love, show me how much you love me," Robin whispered, giving Scott *carte blanche* to do what he wanted.

Scott moved away from the drawn nipples, making a long wet trail down Robin's quivering six-pack. Scott's desire had reached unprecedented levels as the man who had become the center of his universe gave himself unhesitatingly. Robin was open and willing, spread out in a wanton display of lust, every square inch of his body quivering in anticipation. Scott buried his face in the well-trimmed pubic hair, rubbing his cheeks against Robin's shaft, thick and heavy against his stomach. He licked at the ridges and veins, moving slowly up the underside of Robin's cock, loving the twitch, dipping his tongue into the slit that oozed with drops of clear liquid signaling his readiness. He sucked on the bulbous head, twirling his tongue in ever-widening circles, spearing the slit until Robin cried out, lifting his hips automatically, pushing his cock in as far as possible, begging Scott, "More, baby. Take all of it."

"Love you," Scott managed, despite the mouthful. He pulled Robin in and out of the moist heat, swallowing the silky, smooth flesh all the while humming with pleasure as he did it. He released Robin's shaft with a soft pop, focusing his attention on the heavy balls that he rolled around in his mouth one by one, all the while wrapping his fingers around the stiff prick that jutted away from Robin's body, looking almost painfully hard.

"Scott, love, please…."

Scott moved his attention back to Robin's shaft, taking him in swiftly, knowing it wouldn't be long, and he felt the gush of warm spunk filling his mouth while Robin groaned out his pleasure, fisting Scott's hair and fucking his face with abandon.

"Scott, yes… so good, Jesus Christ, I love you, I love your mouth," Robin was babbling, talking nonstop as he continued to spill into Scott's mouth in stuttering spurts until he was milked dry.

He pulled Scott to his chest, latching onto him with a greedy mouth, savoring his own essence as they tongue-fucked their way to the finish. "God, you are so good at that," Robin huffed, trying to catch his breath.

"I love you, Red."

"I know you do, baby. I love you too."

Robin kissed Scott again, sweeping his inner lips with an exploring tongue, pressing tightly against him as Scott moaned feverishly. Robin could feel Scott's erection and his lover's need in the trembling of his skin as he continued to torture him with hot kisses.

"Please," Scott begged, crawling up and lifting himself toward Robin's mouth. "I need you."

"I'm here, love. Always here for you," Robin growled, engulfing Scott to the hilt. He felt Scott's fingers raking through his curls, clutching his hair tightly as he engaged in the action, trying to go deeper, growling with frustration as Robin continued to torture him with maddening expertise.

"God, I'm so close," Scott warned, protesting loudly when Robin pulled away and reached over to the pile of condoms on the nightstand.

"No, don't stop!"

"Shh, baby," Robin whispered gently, opening the packet and rolling the condom onto Scott's jutting erection. He moved without forethought, not thinking about the enormity of this decision, just doing what felt right. He wanted Scott in the worst way, but he needed him to know how much he cared and how committed he was. Giving himself was the only way he knew how.

Once he had the condom in place, he grabbed the lube and squeezed a healthy portion on his hand, rubbing the latex generously, and he reached for Scott. Scott was too far gone to realize what was happening; his thoughts only centered on the orgasm that kept slipping out of his reach. "Red, please let me come."

Scott's blond hair fell forward in a soft curtain of silk, and his eyes were closed as he waited for Robin to decide how he wanted to finish this off.

"Scott, look at me," Robin commanded.

Scott opened his eyes and stared down at Robin, deep blue eyes almost black with lust and comprehension finally dawned on Scott. "Red?"

"Fuck me, love."

"What?"

Robin moved, spreading his legs wider and lifting his hips toward Scott. "Make me yours."

"Yes," Scott's voice cracked as the thought took hold. He lifted one of Robin's legs onto his right shoulder, all the while positioning his cock against the dimple that quivered in anticipation of the onslaught, "Are you sure, Red?"

"So sure, baby."

A sob escaped out of Scott's throat as he readied himself, just before he bent down and planted Robin with a hungry kiss. He pushed, breaching the virgin rings, impaling his lover forcefully. Robin's quick intake of breath changed to a low moan as Scott adjusted, moving his hips slowly, giving Robin a few minutes to accommodate to the fullness. "Okay, Red?"

"Oh my God," Robin whispered, "you're huge!"

"Hurt?"

"A good hurt, love. Don't stop!"

Scott moved Robin's other leg, placing it on his left shoulder, lifting his hips off the bed, pushing in balls-deep until the tip of his cock brushed Robin's gland. The look of surprise on his lover's face was worth all the months of waiting as Scott began to batter him in earnest, relishing the guttural cries that were coming out of Robin's throat with each thrust. "I love you," Scott murmured in a voice filled with emotion as he willed his orgasm away so he could give Red the ride of his life.

He undulated and rolled, moving his hips expertly, pulling all the way out only to push back in forcefully, hitting Robin's prostate over and over, loving the way Robin looked at him in wonder as he continued to pleasure him in a multitude of ways. "Feel good, Red?"

"Like the Fourth of July, baby."

Scott stopped in mid-thrust and smiled down at his lover, "Fireworks, huh?"

"The best." Robin smiled, almost drunk with pleasure. He pulled Scott's ass forward with two hands, even as he bucked against him. "I want you to come," Robin said, holding Scott's golden body close.

"Come with me," Scott whispered, wrapping his fingers around Robin's cock, which was impossibly hard again.

"Yes," Robin answered, finally losing all control as he focused on the hand wrapped around his cock and the thickness stretching him mercilessly. He had never felt so fulfilled despite relinquishing every bit of control.

"You're mine," Robin whispered as the orgasm slowly crept up his body.

"Always!" Scott huffed, giving up the last vestige of restraint as his come poured hot and heavy into the head of the condom even as Robin's climax tore through him, causing him to spasm against Scott and spew hot spunk all over his chest.

They lay in each other's arms for several minutes, trying to wrap their heads around what just happened. Scott was honored that he'd been Robin's first. He never thought his lover would give it up for him, yet he'd gifted him with his virginity, relinquishing control for the first time in their five-month relationship. The power of that gift was immeasurable, and Scott knew that he would forever be attached to the man underneath him. He had given him his heart and body fully, showing him in no uncertain terms how much he was loved.

Robin held Scott, listening to his heartbeat slowly returning to normal. He had never felt this kind of closeness to anyone, and even though a huge part of him was freaking out over the loss of control, the lover in him gloried in what had just transpired between them. He thought of Denise's words, about how love wasn't about giving up power, how it was all about sharing, and he'd never truly understood it until now. He knew that it would take an act of God to separate him from Scott. There was no way in hell he'd give him up voluntarily, and he was willing to fight Scott's inner and outer demons to retain what was his.

SUSIE was in the laboratory placing the last of the soiled instruments into the sterilizer. They'd just finished another complex sinus lift, which had lasted over two hours. The patient was an older gentleman who'd been without teeth for years, and the thought of being able to bite into an apple or eat peanuts again, without have bits and pieces stuck underneath his denture, had given him the courage and will to come up with the money for a full-mouth reconstruction. It would take many months and thousands of dollars, but by the time they were done with him, he'd have a functioning dentition that would allow him to eat whatever he felt like.

This was the part of her job that Susie enjoyed, seeing the look of happiness on a patient's face after they'd done their best to get that person one step closer to their goal.

Scott came into the lab and was leaning against the door, killing time and watching Susie clean up. He was still walking on clouds from his evening with Robin, and today's successful surgery was the cherry on the sundae.

Robin walked in just then with a tray full of dirty instruments, and seeing that Susie was the only person in the lab, he moved close to Scott and brushed him lightly on the lips. "Love you, baby."

Scott smiled gently while reaching up to caress his lover's face, when all of a sudden, Susie stepped in between them and whispered, "Give me a hug, quick."

Both men wrapped their arms around Susie, and she squealed, "Yay, group hugs!"

Jenna watched them from the entrance, having walked into their little scene seconds after Scott had touched Robin's cheek. She didn't see that part, she just saw them looking at each other intently, and when Susie's peripheral vision caught a glimpse of blue, she moved automatically, not knowing who was at the door, only knowing she had to protect both men from censure.

Jenna couldn't figure out what was going on. She felt that something was amiss but couldn't put her finger on it; even though her instincts told her they were up to no good and were putting on a show for her benefit.

"You guys need to hurry up. There are two patients waiting," she said, falling back into her bitch persona since she didn't have any other reason to reprimand them. She'd figure it out eventually, but in the meantime she'd leave it alone and just make sure they were doing their jobs.

"What the fuck, you guys?" Susie said, breathing a sigh of relief when Jenna walked out.

"Sorry, Suz," Scott said, feeling foolish that he'd let his guard down for one second and had gotten caught.

"My fault," Robin interjected. "Can't keep my hands off him," he said, grinning at his lover.

"You two need to cool it, or we'll all be in trouble," Susie scolded.

"Cooling," Robin said as he walked out the door.

Scott smiled as he watched Robin leave the room even though Susie glared at him. "Have you heard a word I've said?"

"What?" Scott asked, turning to her with a besotted look on his face.

"Oh, man, you've got it really bad, huh?"

"You don't know the half of it, Sue. I'm crazy about him."

"I think you're both insane, if you want to know the truth. Keep this up, and Morris will find out, especially now that his pit bull suspects something."

"It's all good," Scott said, tapping her on the shoulder. "I promise to behave."

"And if I believed that, I'd be married with children."

"You're such a cynic."

"Someone's got to be. You two are so sweet I'm getting a fucking toothache."

Scott laughed out loud, too caught up in his love for Robin to really think about anything Susie had to say.

Chapter 23

ROBIN was sitting on his favorite stone bench in Union Square, finishing up his lunch of a chicken salad sandwich and a mango smoothie. He took his last bite and tossed the wrapper into the waste can that was close by. He saw Susie walking across the square and waved at her, hoping to catch her attention as she made her way back to the office, carrying her usual iced coffee from Starbucks.

"What's going on, girl?" he asked, when she finally caught up to him.

"Bored out of my mind," she replied. She had sunglasses on, so Robin couldn't see her eyes, but he could tell by the tone of her voice that she was miserable. He tugged on her hand and waited while she plopped down on the bench, stretching out her long legs in front of her. "I'm in desperate need of entertainment," she said.

"Of the male variety?"

"How'd you guess?"

"It's one of the things we have in common," Robin acknowledged with a grin. "What about your stock broker? I thought that was going well."

"Jon is a nice guy, but not for me."

Robin took her hand and gave it a little squeeze, pleased when she didn't pull away. It had been several months since they'd met, and the level of comfort had built up gradually between them. The fact that he and Scott were crazy in love helped to raise his estimation in her eyes. "What is it you're looking for?" he asked, sincerely interested.

She pushed the sunglasses up on her head and turned to him, fixing her sad brown eyes on him and said, "I wish I knew."

"Okay, then let me rephrase that. What is it about relationships that turns you off?"

"I get bored so easily," Susie said in a voice that mirrored her disgust. "I seem to crave the beginning, the newness of having sex with a stranger, but as soon as that wears off, I'm restless and uncomfortable."

"Is it because they offer no challenge?"

"That's a factor. Most of the men I've been with think I'm some sort of freak."

"Why? Do you bay at the windows at night and turn into a werewolf?"

Susie laughed, finally letting go of the tension that she had wrapped around her like a straightjacket. "If only it were that simple."

"What is it then?"

"I'm looking for a challenge in a man, someone who'll push a button, but the problem is I don't know what that button is."

"I have boxes and boxes filled with buttons," Robin stated. "If you're into kink, I can so relate."

"Kink?"

"Have you ever heard of BDSM?"

"Of course I have, although my knowledge is quite sketchy."

"Have you ever explored that lifestyle?"

"I hate to admit it, Robin, but I haven't."

"That's nothing to be ashamed of. Most people shy away from it because of fear or misconceptions."

Susie looked more interested and animated than she had earlier, and she turned to him and asked, "What is it, exactly?"

"BDSM stands for bondage, domination, sadism, and masochism. It's an acronym describing a lifestyle that a surprisingly large number of people are into."

"Are you?"

"Yes."

"And Scott?" she asked, almost holding her breath.

Robin nodded an affirmative.

"How come I didn't know this?" she pouted, looking like a kid that had missed out on a good birthday party.

"Maybe because he was worried that you'd think he was a deviant."

"Oh, please." She sighed. "Scott knows more shit about me than anyone. I'm the freak, not him."

"How so?"

"Well, I seem to wear out my men for one thing. And if I suggest something remotely kinky, they think I'm some sort of pervert."

"What kind of kinky?"

"Ropes and handcuffs. They always want to tie me down, but when I'm the one that wants to be in charge they head for the hills."

"So you've always had a need to be in complete control of a sexual relationship?"

Susie's cheeks pinked at the suggestion. "Yes."

"Does it involve a need to be physically in control and make your partner suffer a little or do things they'd never dream of doing on their own?"

"Most men balk at all my suggestions."

"That's because you're asking the wrong men, girl."

"Really?"

"Susie, my dear, I think it's time to take you on a little tour."

"A tour?"

"I'm going to introduce you to a friend of mine who's a regular at a BDSM club in this fine city of ours. She's a Dominatrix of the highest caliber."

"What is a Dominatrix?"

"She's the dominating partner in a sadomasochistic relationship."

"Oh. There's a word for women like me?"

Robin laughed at her innocence. "Honey, there's not only a word, there's an entire wardrobe."

"When can we do this?" Susie asked, desperate to see what he was talking about.

"Let me talk to Scott tonight. Maybe we can plan something for Friday, if that works for you."

"Any time, Robin. Just say the word."

"Okay, sweetie. We'll get something going and find you that happy ending you *so* need. Trust me, okay?"

She gave him a tight hug and a loud kiss on the cheek. "I do, thank you."

"You're welcome. Now, let's go back to work."

SUNDAY loomed ahead. It had taken on gigantic proportions in Scott's head as he thought about the scene he and Robin were about to do. This would be another first for them in a week of firsts.

They'd talked about the pros and cons of playing out their fantasy at the office, acknowledging that they would be better off elsewhere, except they needed the props to complete their vision of being ravaged in a dental chair.

"You would have to have a fantasy that involved dentistry. How one track are you?" Robin teased.

"Hey, didn't you say you had the same fantasy? I'm not the only one who's got a one-track mind."

"Maybe we should rethink this," Scott said. They were sitting at their favorite Indian restaurant, not really worried about bumping into Ron since his taste in food was almost as boring as he was. The day that Ron Morris put anything in his mouth that he couldn't pronounce would be the day he gave his blessing to same-sex marriage.

"The odds are in our favor that no one will find out. No one ever goes to work on Sunday, especially not Ron. He's too busy kneeling in church, praying for our lost souls," Robin scoffed.

"I know. Let's do it."

"Yeah?" Robin's grin was contagious, and Scott nodded, unable to keep the smile off his face.

"I get to be the doctor," Robin said.

"What should I wear?" Scott asked.

"I want you to wear something sexy."

"Like what?"

"Surprise me. Let's meet at the office around two o'clock. That will give us time to have our normal Sunday brunch. I'll leave your place around noon and go home and change. Okay?"

"Okay."

"I had a little chat with Susie today," Robin stated, thinking now would be a good time to broach the subject.

"What about?"

"BDSM."

"No!"

"Scott, she's lost. I can't believe you never told her about the lifestyle."

"I never thought she'd be interested."

"She's an obvious Domme, Scott. Can't you see that?"

"No. I don't usually think about Susie and sex at the same time."

"Well, I had a very long conversation with her today, and I told her a little bit about the lifestyle. She seemed more than eager to explore it."

"Did you tell her we were into it?"

"Yes."

"Was she shocked?" Scott asked, surprised that Robin had divulged their little secret.

"No, I believe she was a little jealous and annoyed that you never told her about it."

"Shit!"

"It's all good, love. She knows how uptight you can get."

"I am not uptight!" Scott protested.

"Hey." Robin placed his hand on Scott's neck and pulled him forward gently. He kissed him on the lips and said, "You are uptight as fuck, but I love you anyhow."

"I can't help it," Scott said.

"I'm working on loosening you up, baby. No worries."

"So what exactly did you talk about?" Scott asked, moving back in his seat.

"I told her that we'd take her to a club. I want to introduce her to my friend Anya."

"Who's she?"

"She and I went to Dom school together. She's got amazing skills and mad powers of persuasion. I think Susie would enjoy watching her in action."

"When did you plan on doing this?"

"I told Susie I'd check with you first, but I thought we could do it this Friday if you didn't have any plans."

"That's fine with me."

"Good." Robin reached for a piece of naan out of the basket and bit into it. He chewed slowly, enjoying the freshly baked taste. "I need to go and visit my mom soon. My hair's too long."

"It's nice like that," Scott envisioned himself clutching at the curls in an orgasmic haze.

"I know you like something to hold onto, love, but this is ridiculous. I can barely get my brush through the tangles."

"Do you want to go this Saturday? We can drive there in the morning and be back for dinner."

"Do you mind?" Robin asked, always reluctant to ask Scott for a ride. He didn't want to impose or presume that he had any rights to Scott's vehicle.

"You know how much I enjoy your mother's company. It'll be nice to see her."

"Thank you. I'll let her know we're coming."

Chapter 24

SUSIE had dressed in skintight black pants, stiletto heels, and a red leather bustier that she'd bought only last week. Her hair was parted in the center, framing her face in spun gold. Her lips were glossed a deep berry while her eyelids were darkened in charcoal, making her look exotic and untouchable.

She stood in between Scott and Robin, watching a scene in one of the rooms at the club they'd come to visit. It was situated on the border between San Francisco and Daly City in a three-story building off Camino Real. From the outside, it looked nondescript: an office building no one would look at twice.

Inside though, it was home to one of the kinkiest, members-only, hetero BDSM clubs in the vicinity. Robin gained entrance because of his association through the Society of Dominants he'd trained with. There were rooms on each floor with every variety of tool known in the world. The resident Doms and Dominants were few, thus the need for appointments and exclusivity. Robin had called his friend, Anya, and they were given passes for the night.

Anya had turned out to be quite a revelation. For one thing, she was an Amazon of a woman, easily six feet tall with a body that belonged on a hooker who had decided to take up boxing as a hobby. She was all muscle and curves, tanned a deep brown from her daily sessions within the booth. Her body glistened with oil that accentuated the ripple and flow of muscle on her arms and legs. Her store-bought boobs were encased in black leather straps that barely covered her nipples. She wore thigh-high boots over fishnet stockings that were connected to a black leather G-string that left hardly anything to the imagination. Her ass cheeks were nicely rounded, and her pubic area was completely shaved, giving her the appearance of a pre-pubescent girl, a big turn-on for lots of men.

Aside from the body and the magnificent silver hair that flowed down her back, Anya seduced her clients with eyes that were a translucent pale blue, making her appear almost inhuman. Her eyes could creep people out and mesmerize all at the same time.

She'd embraced Robin like an old friend, easily picking him up off the floor and spinning him around.

"Anya, sweetheart, put me down or these people will think I've gone straight."

"Hah! You? Never," Anya teased, giving Robin a resounding kiss. "Who are these beautiful people with you?"

"This is Scott, my partner and contracted sub, and our friend, Susie."

"I see," Anya replied in a voice that was gravely and very sexy, which probably added to her allure. "Your Dom is one of the best I've ever been with," Anya told Scott.

"I know," Scott acknowledged, beaming at Robin with pride.

"And Susie? Are you here to observe or partake?"

"To observe, right now," Susie replied, never taking her eyes off Anya's face.

"Straight or gay?"

"I'm straight."

"And a woman after my own heart, if my guess is right. Would you like to see a grown man beg?"

"Yes," Susie replied, her breath speeding up with excitement.

"Bound and gagged, his cock leaking with excitement for your touch?"

Susie nodded, unable to reply due to the feelings that were bouncing around her body. She was almost shaking with thoughts of what was to come.

"Gentlemen," Anya addressed Scott and Robin. "Can you find something to amuse yourselves with while I give Susie a guided tour?"

"Absolutely," Robin said. "Is it okay to request a private room?"

"I've already reserved one for you."

"You're so thoughtful, Anya," Robin acknowledged.

She laughed and shook her head. "No, I'm not. I'm just watching out for my members who have no desire to watch man-on-man sex."

"Such prudes," Robin said with an eye roll.

Anya stepped forward and gave Robin a quick peck on the lips. "Take your man and have fun with him."

"I will. Watch out for our girl. She's looking for something."

"I've got her safely in hand," Anya replied, looking every bit in control.

"No doubt," Robin answered.

"Well, she's interesting," Scott admitted once Anya and Susie left the room.

"She can wield a whip like you won't believe."

"I'd like to watch her someday. You think she'll help Susie?"

"If anyone can, she will. I have a feeling that tonight will change Susie's life."

"I wish her luck. I know that the first time I walked into a club I felt like I'd been given the keys to heaven."

"Amen to that," Robin agreed, taking Scott's hand and getting into the elevator. Their room was on the third floor, and they rode up silently, only to step out onto a carpeted corridor that was so quiet the only sound they heard was their own breathing.

The room they'd been assigned was a typical room with the requisite spanking bench, flogging cross, and four-poster bed. There was a cabinet with an assortment of tools that gave Robin pause as he perused the contents. "Scott, take off your clothes." Robin had his back turned to Scott, and his voice had shifted slightly, moving into his Dom space. Being in the club and in this room made it an easy transition.

When he turned around, he was holding a wand with a big globe attached to it that caused Scott's breathing to accelerate the minute he laid eyes on it.

"We'll be using this tonight," Robin stated, not asking, just letting Scott know.

"Yes, Master," Scott answered softly, already resting in display position, his hands clasped behind his back, his eyes lowered respectfully.

"Have you ever used a violet wand?"

"No, Sir."

"Really? I'm surprised, but delighted! I like being the first." Robin put the wand down on the table beside the bed and took off his shirt and pants. He left his briefs on for the moment.

"Get on the bed and spread out. I'm going to cuff and blindfold you."

Scott moved to the bed silently, watching Robin the entire time. His cock had begun to harden as soon as he saw the violet wand and continued to grow with every command that came out of Robin's mouth.

He lay on the bed and spread eagle, waiting for Robin to place his restraints. He felt the soft leather cuffs that Robin secured expertly, attaching them to the hooks at the end of the chains on the four corners of the bed.

"Are you comfortable?" Robin asked, passing his hand over Scott's chest and pausing at the nipple ring so he could tug on it, eliciting a yelp from Scott but noting with some satisfaction that his erection only increased in dimension. "My slut boy," he whispered, completely aroused by his sub's responsive nature.

"Master," Scott whispered.

"What, baby?"

"Touch me."

"Be patient, my love. No rushing this."

Scott whimpered and moved his hips, even as his cock twitched and lay heavy against his stomach. He was silenced by a hungry kiss as Robin sucked on his tongue, probing his mouth relentlessly. "Tonight I'm going to make you scream, baby."

"Please...."

"Shhh... relax and enjoy, love."

Robin took a fur-lined blindfold and covered Scott's eyes, fastening the binding securely. "Can you see?"

"No, Sir."

"Is anything pulling?"

"No, Master," Scott said, his voice low and aching with need.

Robin moved over to pick up the wand and turned it on, the electric current pulsing through it quietly, lighting the bulb a brilliant violet color, thus the name. He ran the wand over his forearm, relishing the tingling sensation it caused. He knew that this same sensation was increased a hundredfold when the wand was passed along more sensitive areas of the body such as the penis or the scrotum. He would start with the globe attachment and switch to the rake after a few minutes, allowing Scott to adjust to the sensation. The rake was more intense and he was saving it for the end.

"I don't want you to come until I tell you," Robin ordered.

"Yes, Master."

"We begin then," Robin said gently, taking the wand and switching it to the lowest setting. He wanted to make sure that Scott was comfortable in every way. He swept the wand across Scott's nipples, moving it back and forth, about two inches away from the skin. The trick was not to pull back too far, or the electrical arc would break; however, too close would do the same thing. It had to be positioned perfectly to create the sensation that could only be described as a tingling sting.

"Master…." Scott moaned.

"Good, baby?"

"Yes." Scott was trying hard not to beg, but the writhing of his hips was a clear indication of his state of mind. Robin's own erection pressed hard against his briefs, and the wet spot beginning to spread was evidence of his need.

"You like this, love?"

"Yes, please, more."

Robin moved the wand lower, flipping the switch up a notch, hovering around Scott's cock, which seemed to twitch and want to follow the sensation for as long as possible. Scott moaned loudly, lifting his hips off the bed.

"Oh… God…."

Robin moved his hand up to Scott's nipple and pulled on the ring even as the wand got closer to Scott's balls, causing Scott to spread his legs further apart. "Master," he said in a strangled voice, lifting his head off the pillow with this last move. "Please touch my cock."

"No, love. Not yet."

Scott was starting to tremble, the spasms rippling through his skin in waves, and Robin decided to switch to the rake, making sure that the level of electricity was pushed up another notch. Scott was completely in the dark as to what was going on, and when he felt a new sensation, he had no idea that the attachment now looked like a miniature garden rake with three tines that created pleasure that made him scream, and the scream changed to a keening that got Robin right in the gut, making him stop for a second to pull off his briefs as his cock popped free.

"Master… please, oh, God… make this stop."

"Use your safe word if you need it, love."

"No, oh, no… I want to come… please touch me."

Robin held the wand with one hand, and he pulled at his cock with the other, pinching the head to try and stem the inevitable. The noises coming out of Scott's throat were making this unbearably erotic for Robin, and he was hard pressed not to throw the wand aside and plunge his cock into Scott's hole which was on display so wantonly.

He moved the wand over and around Scott's balls, pointing the tines at his cock, close to but never touching the skin. Scott was bucking his hips off the bed, moaning incoherently, switching to a pitiful begging sound that finally got to Robin.

"I'm going to let you come, baby," he growled, unable to hold off any longer. He put the wand down and took Scott in his mouth, and his sub shot streams of hot come down his Dom's throat, crying out his name nonstop.

"Master… Sir… I love you, love you… love you!"

And when Scott was finally spent and lay boneless on the bed, Robin took his own aching cock and rolled a condom on it. He slicked it up with lube and positioned himself in front of his sub, parting his legs unceremoniously, and he plunged, impaling Scott, extracting another scream out of him when he pegged his gland, fulfilling his promise to make this a night of firsts.

Chapter 25

SUSIE was silent as they made their way back to San Francisco. It was late, and the streets were fairly deserted, which made the trip back into the city a breeze. She hadn't said a word since they got into the car, so Robin and Scott didn't say much either, their thoughts filled with the scene they'd just played out. Scott reached across the console to touch Robin, and he felt the warm hand slip into his and give it a gentle squeeze.

"Scott?"

Scott looked up into the rearview mirror and saw Susie was looking into it as well. Their eyes met and held, pregnant with unspoken questions. "What is it, Suz?"

"Can we go to your place first? I'm not ready to go home yet."

Scott looked over at Robin, who nodded quickly and said, "Of course."

They got to Scott's building in no time, parked the car, and rode the elevator silently to his floor. As soon as they got into the apartment and turned on the lights, Scott went over to the small bar in the living room and poured them all a drink. No one seemed to object when he handed them the glasses of vodka.

Susie sat on the sofa opposite the two men and took a hefty swallow.

"I'm a little overwhelmed by what just happened," she said, finally breaking her silence.

"Were you shocked by what Anya was doing to her subs?" Robin asked, leaning forward and resting his elbows on his legs. He was watching Susie intently, trying to gauge her state of mind.

"I was shocked by my feelings," Susie said bluntly.

Robin stood and went to sit beside her. He held her hand in a show of support and asked, "Were you excited by watching the scenes?"

"Yes," she whispered, "what's wrong with me, Robin? Why was I so aroused by the sight of grown men groveling at Anya's feet? I should have been horrified by what she was doing, but I wasn't. The sound of the whip snapping and hitting them on the back was making me horny. Their begging to be allowed to climax was the most erotic thing I've ever heard."

"You're a natural Domme, sweetie. It's who you are."

"Am I sick?" Susie's eyes welled with tears suddenly, "What kind of person gets off on shit like this?"

"You'd be surprised at how many do."

"Maybe I should see a shrink?" Susie turned to Scott looking for answers. He could tell she was terrified by her feelings, much like he was the first time he realized he was into pain.

"You don't need a shrink," Scott said gently, making his way over to her side. He took her in his arms and held her tightly, feeling her trembling against his chest. "It's going to be okay, Suz. I know what you're thinking because I've been there."

She pulled away from Scott and looked at both men with haunted eyes. "Am I some sort of sexual deviant?"

"No," Robin interjected, tapping her on the arm and pulling her gaze away from Scott's. "There's nothing wrong with you. It's the way you're hard-wired. I'm the same, and I don't consider myself sick or insane. We like what we like."

"Scott?" Susie turned to her friend, waiting for clarification. "Are you?"

"I'm the one that does the begging," Scott answered, a little embarrassed to admit it out loud.

"And you two have this all worked out?" Susie asked, blown away by Scott's revelation.

"Yes."

"All these years I've blamed it on my partners, when all along, I'm the one with issues," she spoke softly, almost as if she were having a conversation with herself.

"Look, there's no need to beat yourself up over this," Scott stressed.

"Really? Were you cheerfully accepting of your kinks when you first realized you were into this sort of thing?"

"To be perfectly honest, I thought I was quite mad," Scott replied.

"Is this part of the reason you were wigging out in Chicago? I bet you were freaked when you realized you weren't only gay, you were into BDSM as well."

"You're right. That had a lot to do with it, but I've worked on my issues. I'm learning to accept who I am, and with Robin's help, I'm getting better each day, as you will."

"And how's that supposed to happen?"

"You can go back to your old life, live in denial, and pretend that tonight never happened, or you can embrace who you are, Susie. There are hundreds, no, make that thousands of people like us. We just don't advertise," Scott replied.

"It is really okay?" she said, finally letting her tears pour down her face. "I'm freaking out here."

"Hey," Robin said gently, pulling her into his embrace. "No need to panic, sweetie. There's always going to be a little bit of fear, but that's what makes it so exciting. Do you want to keep going from man to man like you've been doing, searching for the ultimate high that you will never get in a so-called *normal* relationship?" Robin asked.

"Fuck that. I'm bored out of my mind!"

"Precisely! Anya will open up a whole new world for you."

"I'm not going to prostitute myself." Susie was adamant.

"Anya is not a prostitute," Robin said seriously.

"Doesn't she sleep with her clients?"

"Anya is a Dominatrix for hire, but that doesn't include sex."

"You can say no?"

"Susie, a pro Domme is not a whore. They're hired for their ability to indulge in a man's secret fantasy through whatever form of kink is required. Some men just want to be whipped; others need to be tied down and humiliated, to role-play, to be degraded. The world is your oyster, my dear. There is no kink or fetish that's too outlandish or hasn't been done before; however, the big difference between the BDSM world and prostitution is that whatever goes on between Domme and client is completely consensual, and sex only enters into the equation if both parties want it. Anya only sleeps with partners of her choice. Right now, I believe she has a contracted sub and only sleeps with him."

"What does a contracted sub mean?"

"She's in a physical relationship with a submissive who is committed to her exclusively for a certain period of time. Contracts can last anywhere from six months to several years."

"Like a marriage?"

"I wouldn't call it that. Unlike marriage, a contracted relationship has an end in sight and is renewable. People stay together because they want to, because their mutual needs are being fulfilled."

"Marriage should be renewable, don't you think?" Susie asked with a smirk. "It would make people think twice about the way they treated each other."

"Spoken as a witness to some pretty shitty marriages," Robin stated.

"You don't know the half of it."

"No, I don't. But I do know that there is hope for you, of finding a good and rewarding relationship in the BDSM world, Susie."

"I have no idea what that's like, to be with someone who shares my kinks."

"There is nothing more satisfying and fulfilling than finding the perfect submissive who will give you what you're looking for."

"Have you and Scott found that perfect relationship?" she asked, looking at her friends with a whole new perspective.

"Yes," they replied in unison, smiling broadly. Scott reached for Robin and wrapped an arm around his neck and kissed him deeply.

"Wow, you two are making me jealous."

"Don't be jealous. Think of this as a goal you can easily reach if you let go of your fears and put your trust in your true feelings," Robin stated. "Do you want me to set up another meeting with Anya?"

"Will she even want to be bothered with me? Why can't you teach me, Robin? Aren't you a Dom?"

"I went to school to learn how to be a good Dom. That's where I met Anya."

"There's an actual school for this?"

"Well, not a school in the true sense of the word. You won't find it listed in America's top one hundred colleges, but there are courses that are given in the industry that will teach you how to use your tools and how to be a safe and responsible Dominatrix. It's not as simple or as easy as you think."

"No, I'm sure it's not. How would I go about doing this?"

"Anya is a good source. She'll hook you up with the right people."

"I'd like to think about it," Susie replied. "Where do you and Scott do your thing?"

"It's called a scene, Susie, and we have a playroom right here in this apartment."

"Can I see it?" she asked, more and more curious.

Scott stood and pulled her up with one hand. "Follow us."

They walked down the hallway and entered the room they'd converted into their playroom. The whipping post and spanking bench dominated the room. There were chains hanging from the ceiling, and a row of whips were secured in a dark wooden shelf with slots for each one. Susie gravitated to the display and ran her hands lovingly on the leather handles. She opened the doors of the tall bureau off to one side of the room and scanned the contents. It was a smorgasbord of toys, tools for pleasure and pain, many she'd never seen before.

She turned to Robin and said, "Wow."

He grinned. "Pretty exciting stuff, huh?"

"No kidding. Have you used all of these?"

"Most of them."

She picked up a leather harness that looked like a small basket, "What's this?"

"It's a chastity belt of sorts. You position it around a cock to prevent orgasm."

"Uh huh. And this?" Susie held up a spreader bar.

"It's attached to your ankles to prevent any movement during a whipping."

"I see."

"There are as many toys as there are kinks, Suz."

"I'm beginning to realize that more and more," Susie admitted. "Robin, I think I'd like to set up that meeting with Anya."

"Good. I know that you won't regret it."

"And now, I'll let you gentlemen take me home."

"Have you seen enough?" Scott asked.

"For the time being."

They walked out of the room, and Susie grabbed her purse. They made their way out of the apartment and back down to the garage. In the car, on the way to Susie's apartment, Scott asked, "Are you still seeing Jon?"

"Yes, but it's nothing formal. We hook up when we feel like it, although he does want more."

"You'll have a whole array of men to choose from when you get into the scene," Robin said. "Your choices will blow your mind."

"Thank you both for being so honest," Susie spoke, grateful for their friendship. "I know this couldn't have been easy for you, Scott. You've always been such a private person."

"You're welcome, Suz. Robin and I just want you to be happy."

"I think that I'm headed in the right direction," she said, heartened by the discoveries of the evening.

Chapter 26

SATURDAY morning shone bright with promise, another beautiful spring day in San Francisco. Scott stood on the balcony of his apartment looking out at the sailboats and larger ships, all vying for a place in the deep waters that made up the natural harbor that was the gateway to this city by the bay.

He felt a hand snaking around his waist and light kisses fluttering around his neck, raising goose bumps all over his skin. He leaned back against Robin and lifted a hand to his cheek, and then he turned and embraced him, pressing hard against the lean body that moved strong hands down his back, resting on his ass cheeks, pulling him closer.

"Good morning, love," Robin whispered in a voice so tantalizingly sexy.

"Morning, Sir. You want some breakfast?"

"Why don't we just grab something on our way to San Ramon?"

"That sounds good," Scott answered, always happy when he didn't have to prepare a meal.

"Let's forgo breakfast and move straight to brunch; stop at Trader Vic's and have Bloody Marys? They open at eleven-thirty. It's a gorgeous day, and we can sit out on the deck, get some sun, people watch," Robin cajoled, trying to get Scott in the mood.

"Do you think it's okay?"

"Scott, Ron hardly ever leaves the city unless he's going fishing, and the last time I looked, the only fish in Emeryville were fried or sautéed on the daily special."

"Not true. What about the fish in the bay?"

"Baby, Ron is a fly fisherman, not a deep-sea guy."

"Okay."

"Okay?" Robin tried not to get overly excited by the small victory. Every time he got Scott close to letting his guard down, he'd rethink the plan and imagine all the worst-case scenarios, only to back out of an outing, opting for the safety of their apartment.

"Yes, but you have to be on your best behavior," Scott teased. "No groping me under the table."

"Oh, you're no fun at all, love."

"Promise me."

"I will. Promise," Robin said, making a cross over his heart. He loved the way Scott looked early in the morning before he put on his public face. He looked ten years younger and innocent as hell when his silky blond hair fell loosely around his forehead. Robin preferred it when he left it natural, but he rarely did at work, styling it so that the hair stayed out of his eyes and away from his face, making him look more mature and responsible. He hadn't shaved yet, so there was that light layer of blond stubble that was always wonderfully scratchy when it rubbed again his neck.

"You look gorgeous this morning, love. Your eyes are like candy," Robin muttered, "green Life Savers."

Scott laughed and kissed him quickly on the lips. "You always say the nicest things."

"Hey! That was a compliment," Robin said in mock outrage. He slapped Scott lightly on his bottom and said, "Get that beautiful, tight ass in the shower and hurry up!"

"Yes, Master." Scott grinned, running his tongue around his lips and grabbing his crotch lasciviously.

"Oh, you did *not* just do that," Robin said, narrowing his eyes. "Now you *will* pay." He took Scott's hand and moved off to the bedroom, having every intention of seeing his sub on his knees in record time.

SCOTT watched as Denise moved around Robin, snipping away at the locks that were falling like leaves off a tree.

"Not so short, Mrs. Kennedy."

"Sweetie, you need to stop calling me that. I'm Denise."

Scott felt his cheeks flush and he quickly said, "Please, Denise."

"You need something to hang onto, huh?"

Scott laughed, as charmed by his lover's mother as always. She was one of the most honest and down-to-earth individuals he'd ever met.

"It's important."

"Oh, I'll bet it is." She smirked, jumping a little when Robin tapped her lightly on the arm.

"Behave yourself, Mama."

"I'm behaving!"

"You're embarrassing my partner."

"Oh, so it's official then? Scott is your partner?"

Robin waited to hear what Scott had to say and let out a sigh of relief when he heard the affirmative.

"Yes, he's my partner." Scott glowed, looking at Robin adoringly.

"Good. Now maybe I can get my teeth fixed for free," Denise teased. She smiled when she said it, showing off her beautiful white teeth.

"There's nothing wrong with your teeth, Ma. It's your tongue that's too loose."

"Just having fun, sweetie." She stepped back and appraised the haircut, running her hands through the locks that she'd left a little long, in deference to her son-in-law's request. "How's that, Scott?"

"It's perfect."

"Hello? I'm still here," Robin said, standing and looking in the mirror. "Too long, Mama."

"No, it's not," Scott said.

"I agree with Scott," Denise countered. "It's just fine."

"You guys are ganging up on me."

"We are, aren't we, Scott?" Denise smiled at the shy man her son was in love with.

Scott nodded, and Denise pulled the white cloth off Robin's shoulders and shook it out. "Get the vacuum cleaner, Robin, and pick up all your hair."

"Yes, Madam. You want a tip?"

"Don't be insolent; just take me out to dinner."

"We can do that. Where to?" Robin asked.

"Mexican?"

"Chevys okay, Ma?"

"Goodie!" was all the answer Robin needed.

They opted for the fajitas, which were brought to their table on sizzling platters, piled high with strips of beef, chicken, onions, and green peppers, lightly dusted with Chevys's famous spices. The homemade tortillas completed the dish, and Robin and Denise drowned everything in flaming hot salsa, cooled off by the frozen margaritas in tub-size goblets. Scott elected not to drink, volunteering to be the designated driver for the evening.

It was such a source of pleasure for Scott to be with Robin and his mother in a relaxed and loving atmosphere. His experience with his own adopted parents had been the complete opposite. They were kind and loving folk, but reserved and formal. They were horrified by public gestures of affection and hardly ever voiced an opinion, even if it happened to contradict one of their own. They made it a point to avoid controversy until the day that Scott had admitted he was gay. That was the only time he heard any kind of criticism. And that came loud and clear.

Robin and Denise enjoyed debating over everything. The fine repartee between the two over the state of the economy or the melting ice caps was always a good source of entertainment. Mother and son matched each other wit for wit, and the amazing part in Scott's eyes was that they harbored no anger or resentment if their opinions clashed. The love between the two was almost palpable.

"Scott, sweetheart," Denise said, looking at him pointedly. "You're going to have to learn to butt into our conversations eventually, or you'll lose the ability to speak."

"Give me time." Scott chuckled. "I'm just enjoying watching the two of you."

"You plan on spending the night?" she asked Robin.

"Nah… we've got to head back. Maybe next time."

"Whenever you want, okay?"

"I know, Ma. Thanks."

They dropped her off, engulfing her with kisses and hugs, promising to come back soon. As they pulled away, Robin turned to Scott and said, "Let's go by the club."

"What club?"

"The one I used to work at, where we first met."

"Oh. That club."

"Yeah."

"Why?"

"I want to dance with you in public," Robin said, looking at Scott with eyes that all but begged. "I want the world to see what we have."

"Red."

"Please, love. No one knows who you are. They have no idea what you do or where you live."

Scott looked at Robin and said, "One dance."

"Maybe two?"

Scott gave in, unable to resist such a tender request. "Okay, two."

The club was packed. It was Saturday night, after all, and when they walked in, Robin was greeted like a returning hero. Guys came up to him to shake his hand and pat him on the back, many of them former subs who'd done scenes with him in the past. They were all curious to see the new man in Robin's life. "Are you back for good, Red, or just slumming?"

"No, we're just passing through. I wanted a drink and a dance, for old time's sake."

"How about a scene?" a brunet asked, obviously one of his former clients.

"Not tonight, Joe. I'm in a contract."

"Really? Since when?"

"Since none of your business," Robin smiled, trying to keep it light. He tugged at Scott's hand and led him to the dance floor. They were playing a ballad, which was just as well. Robin was in the mood to hold Scott and nuzzle his neck. "You smell good, love."

"So do you."

They danced for several minutes, and finally Robin pulled away and said, "It could always be like this if you'd come out."

Scott cocked his head, surprised. "I will in three months."

"You know it'll be longer than that."

"Why?"

"Because even if your contract is over and you buy the practice, he'll still be getting income from you for another year, isn't that right?"

"So?"

"So are you really going to tell him you're gay? What do you think he'll do at that point?"

"What can he do legally? Nothing."

"I don't know, Scott. I just don't like the whole idea of you buying into that practice. You're good enough to do this on your own; you'd have patients who'd follow you willingly."

"Why not step into a ready-made practice? Do you have any idea how lucky I am to have this opportunity?"

"Yeah."

"Look, Red," Scott said seriously. "It would take me ten years, at least, to get to where I am right now, and all I have to do is pretend for a few more months."

"It's the principle of the thing, Scott. I can't argue that you're skipping over years of struggle, I just can't stomach the way you're going about it."

"So, what? I'm disgusting you?" Scott asked, stepping away.

"No, baby, no," Robin said, pulling Scott back to him. "Stay here, hold me." His voice was gruff with emotion, but he tried a gentler approach. "I just want you to look in the mirror and like what you're seeing, love. That's all."

"I like me just fine," Scott said stiffly. He was hurt and a little shocked by the turn of the conversation. He had no idea that Robin felt this way about the contract with Ron. Scott knew Robin detested the man and had just assumed Robin was in agreement with his decision. Apparently not.

"Why is this coming up now?" Scott asked, pushing away again and walking off the dance floor. He moved to the exit and made his way across the parking lot, unlocked his car, and waited for Robin to catch up.

"Hey," Robin said as soon as he sat down in the passenger seat.

"What the fuck do you want from me, Robin? Shall I walk away from a four-million-dollar practice because you don't like Ron Morris?"

"No. You walk away because *you* don't like him. Because the lies and the deceit will catch up to you, and one day you'll pay the price."

"What are you talking about?"

"I'm talking about believing in yourself, in your own abilities. You're good, Scott; you don't need Ron's patients, who are, for the most part, straight and steeped in the same world he comes from. Do you think these people will accept who you are once Ron gets done trashing you?"

"Why will he trash me? It's to his advantage that I succeed."

"Because he's a zealot and won't be able to keep his mouth shut!"

"I think you're over thinking this, Robin. I don't believe Ron would deliberately work to destroy everything I've done in one year just because he doesn't like my brand of loving. It would hurt his pocketbook, and I know that's paramount in his life."

Robin ran a hand through his hair, tired of arguing. He knew it was pointless. Scott didn't understand where he was coming from, and he wasn't willing to walk away from Scott. He loved him too much.

"Okay, love, let's drop this. I'm sorry. Maybe I'm wrong and everything will work out," Robin admitted, hoping that Scott could forgive him and put the conversation behind them.

"It's okay," Scott said softly, although a little confused by the sudden flip of the switch. He looked at Robin, questioning, "Do you still want to be with me? In a contract?"

"Absolutely," Robin answered, asking Scott the same question back, desperate for a clear and positive answer. "Don't you?"

"Yes… God, yes," Scott said, reaching for Robin. They held each other for the longest time, reluctant to part and start the drive home.

"Tell me you love me," Scott whispered into Robin's ear.

"I love you, baby. My whole life is yours."

"And mine is yours as well. Can't you see that?"

Robin closed his eyes and said *yes*, even though deep down inside, he worried that one day he might be proven wrong, and Scott would push him away.

Chapter 27

SCOTT stood in front of the office building, wrestling with his decision one final time. He and Robin had discussed it again last night and early this morning, debating the wisdom of their choice. Finally, they'd determined they were both being paranoid, that no one would see them, and that they should do this and get it out of their systems.

They'd even decided not to have sex last night, opting to hold each other instead. A large part of that decision was trying to get past the words exchanged in San Ramon. Scott knew Robin had many doubts about the outcome of his contract with Ron. Deep in his heart, he knew Robin was right, that Ron could still make trouble for him if he found out that he was gay. However, his professional side refused to give his feelings any credence. He chose to believe that once he'd passed the year mark and money had exchanged hands, he would be his own man and therefore able to do as he pleased.

He'd worn tight black jeans, cowboy boots, and a shirt he'd bought long ago at a Western apparel shop. It had the requisite embroidery on the yoke, and the deep green complemented his eyes, making them look even more arresting. He'd deliberately kept the first three buttons open so that his nipple ring was clearly visible. He'd finished off his look with a Stetson and a black leather jacket.

Since it was Sunday, the doorman was missing, and the only one in the lobby was the security guard who barely gave Scott a glance once he showed his ID and signed in.

He entered the office with his key, pausing in the waiting room as if he were a regular patient. Shortly after, the door leading into the actual clinic was pushed open, and Robin stepped through wearing a dark blue lab coat over his street clothes.

He appraised Scott, instantly attracted by the Western look. Scott didn't know that Robin had a thing for men in hats, so his choice of attire couldn't have been more perfect.

"Do you have an appointment?" Robin asked formally.

"I sure do, Doc; got me one hell of an ache."

Robin grinned at the exaggerated twang Scott seemed to have picked up somewhere along the way. "Well, step right in. Mister?"

"Tex. Y'all can call me Tex."

"Right." Robin was disarmed. He signaled for "Tex" to walk ahead of him, because he had every intention of checking out that fine ass encased in jeans that fit like a glove. Scott even walked differently, probably due to the boots that had a two-inch heel, making him swagger a little, seemingly taller than he actually was. When they got to the cubicle normally used for surgical procedures, Robin shut the door behind him and said, "May I take your hat and jacket?"

"Sure thing, doc. Take care of that puppy," Tex drawled, as he handed Robin the Stetson. "I've spent a lot of hard earned money on that hat, and I want to make sure it don't get crushed."

"I'll make sure it's safe, Tex," Robin replied, trying desperately not to laugh and ruin it all. He couldn't believe how easily Scott had slipped into his role.

The jacket came next, and Robin's pheromones kicked into high gear when he saw the open shirt, affording him a glimpse of chest hair and the glint of the golden nipple ring. He could feel the blood rushing to his groin, and he had to reach down and adjust himself to get more comfortable.

"Y'all okay, Doc?" Scott had seen Robin move his hand, and he smiled seductively, lowering his voice and staring at Robin's crotch, seeing the bulge that was making Robin so uncomfortable.

"I'm more than fine, Tex. Now take a load off and sit in this chair so I can have a look at what's causing the pain."

Scott sat on the dental chair and leaned back, crossing his legs one over the other. He'd left his hair free of gel so it fell smoothly over his forehead, and he pushed it back with his right hand, raking his fingers through the soft strands in a nervous gesture.

"Now tell me exactly what hurts, Tex," Robin said pointedly.

"I got this pain, Doc."

"Yeah?"

"I do."

"Where's the pain?" Robin asked, reaching for the bib clips sitting on the tray in front of him. He held the chain that had the two clips attached on either end and let it dangle over Scott's chest, lowering his hand so the clips brushed against the skin, teasing. Robin removed Scott's shirt and let it drop on the floor. He saw that his nipples had puckered into tight nubs, and he smiled wickedly, flicking the nipple ring and tugging on it, hearing Scott's soft hiss of pain. "Does that hurt, Tex?"

"No, Sir. It feels mighty good."

"I think you're just playing with me, Tex."

"How do you figure, Doc?"

"I think you like a little pain, don't you, big guy?"

"I don't rightly know, Doc."

"Let's find out, shall we?" Robin asked, turning on the seductive tone. He waited to see what Scott would do, but when he only nodded his head, Robin proceeded, taking the clips and attaching one end to a nipple. Scott stopped breathing for a minute, holding in his breath while Robin clamped the other nipple in the tight vice, trying not to catch the nipple ring. When Scott started to breathe again in deep, ragged gulps, Robin knew that the pain around the tender skin must have been intense.

"How does that feel now, Tex?"

Scott growled and squirmed in the chair, trying to center himself.

Robin gazed at Scott's crotch and saw the reaction to the stimulus. His cock was clearly outlined as it pressed against his pants.

"I think that you're a bad, bad cowboy playing with your doctor," Robin's voice was deeper and laced with hunger, seducing Scott with his tone even as he tugged on the chain again.

"I'm hurting, Doc."

"Oh, you're just a bad boy playing a naughty game, aren't you?"

"Just need some loving."

"And you think that I can provide that?"

"Yes." The word came out in a gasp as Robin started pulling at Scott's zipper.

"You're right, Tex. I *can* make it all better," Robin's eyes had turned a deep sapphire, burning through Scott as he gazed at him. The progress of the zipper was excruciatingly slow as Robin tortured his sub with his measured movements. Scott never took his eyes off Robin's face, silently pleading for him to hurry and get on with it.

Finally the pants parted, and Scott's cock peeked through, breaking free of its prison. Robin knew Scott would be naked under his pants; his penchant for going commando hadn't changed with the costume. He felt his desire ratchet up at least ten degrees. "You are such a slutty, bad cowboy, tempting your doctor this way. I think you deserve to be punished."

"Yeah...."

Robin took the latex gloves off the tray and tied each of Scott's wrists to the chair handles, using the gloves like ropes. The latex stretched perfectly, and after he made a knot around each wrist, he knew that Scott wasn't going anywhere. He stood and moved over to the black bag sitting in a corner. He dug around and pulled out the red nylon cord that was a part of the fantasy.

"I'm going to tie you down, cowboy. Make you pay for tempting me like this," Robin stated in a voice that left no room for discussion. He moved toward Scott, letting the rope slither through his hands and dangle down to the floor, watching Scott react.

Scott's excitement was building, his erection growing plump and pressing hard against his stomach. He attempted to soothe lips that had gone dry with longing; the tip of his pink tongue licked his mouth, making him look even more desirable. "Fix me, Doc." He'd started to beg.

"Oh, I'll fix you, all right. By the time I'm done with you, you'll be hard-pressed to sit on a horse."

"What are you going to do, Doc?"

"I'm going to ride you, cowboy." Robin's voice was steely with determination. "I'm going to fuck that hurt right out of you, right here in this chair, but first, a taste of my belt to remind you not to toy with my feelings. Show you who's in charge here."

"Sir!"

"Oh, don't pretend this isn't what you've been hankering for since you walked through that door." Robin dismissed Scott's protest with a wave of his hand, pausing at the foot of the chair; taking note of Scott's quickened breathing and heightened skin color. He pulled off Scott's boots, socks, and pants and threw everything off to the corner in a messy pile.

"Spread those legs," he commanded forcefully, delighted to see that Scott's erection hadn't weakened in the slightest. Robin could practically taste the moisture oozing out of Scott's slit, dotting the plump head.

"Doc, please, touch me."

"No."

He wound the rope around Scott's waist, crisscrossing it over his chest and the back of the chair, imprisoning him. It was every bit as glorious as he imagined, seeing Scott's golden skin against the red rope, his legs splayed wantonly displaying himself. His shaft lay thick against his stomach, and it twitched when Robin pulled his leather belt from his pants and wound it tightly around his right hand. Scott was powerless to look away, mesmerized by the sight of his master getting ready to proceed with his brand of loving. Robin lifted his hand and brought the belt down forcefully, catching Scott on his thigh. He closed his eyes when he heard the slap of the leather against Scott's skin and his cry of pain. The loud groan was all it took for Robin's cock to respond, pushing hard against his jeans.

"You like that, slut boy?"

Scott gasped as Robin's arm came down again, raising a welt on his other thigh. His tried to lift his hips off the chair but was unable to, trapped by the rope.

"You're not going anywhere, cowboy. Sit back and enjoy the ride."

Robin hit him again, making several stripes down his legs, relishing the cries that were now turning into deep moans as Scott slowly moved into subspace.

"Tell me what you want, Tex."

"Please—" Scott's voice cracked. He was flying high as the pain slowly switched to pleasure of the highest order, shifting him deeply into subspace. Robin put the belt down when he saw the look of rapture on his sub's face, and he moved slowly and touched Scott's leg, now lined with red welts. It was hot to the touch, and Robin caressed him gently, moving his hand up to Scott's groin, which looked painfully hard.

"Feel good, cowboy?"

"Yes," Scott replied automatically, his body on fire, desperate to come.

Robin shoved his pants out of the way, freeing up the erection that pulled away from his body. "I'm going to ride you, cowboy," he growled, determined to see this through to the glorious end. "I'm going to ride you hard and put you away wet with my come, got that?"

Scott moaned, moving his head back and forth, clenching and unclenching his hands as they ached to touch, to relieve the pressure that had built to the breaking point. "Please," he begged, exciting Robin even further.

Robin knelt at the foot of the chair, spreading Scott's thighs and bending his knees. He grabbed a condom that he'd placed on the instrument tray earlier and rolled it onto his cock, slicking himself with the K-Y Jelly that he'd brought along for good measure. "You ready for me, Tex?"

Scott responded with a cry, lifting his hips as much as he could, bracing his feet against the chair, readying himself for the push. Robin moved and shoved his cock into Scott forcefully, pushing hard as they both grunted, the smell of their arousal filling the air.

"You're a slut." Robin huffed, thrusting in and out of Scott's tight ass, never taking his eyes off his lover. "You like that, bad boy?"

"Yes… yes… fuck me hard… Doc…."

"Like that?" Robin asked, undulating in slow tortuous moves, prodding Scott's gland. He couldn't take his eyes off Scott's face as he thrust in and out. He was bound to his man as surely as the rope that twisted around him, enthralled by the beauty of his submission as he gave himself over completely to the pleasure that wracked his body. Scott was deep in subspace.

"Open your eyes," Robin commanded, wanting to see the love that poured out of his sub as he climaxed.

"Doc…."

"Who's your master, slut boy?"

"You are," Scott replied, his moaning turning frantic as he chased the fire that coursed through him, singeing every nerve ending.

"Are you mine?"

"Yes!"

"Show me, my love. Come for me."

Scott broke when he heard Robin call him *love.* His orgasm swept through him, starting at the tip of his curled toes, moving swiftly up his body until it exploded out his head. He cried out when he felt Robin shudder and bite down on his shoulder, the pain intertwined so easily with the pleasure, taking them both on the ride of their lives.

It seemed to go on forever, the warm come splashing against Robin's chest and stomach, adding to his pleasure as the room filled with Scott's scent.

"I love you," Robin cried out, his voice shaky with emotion.

Scott was in a trance but answered immediately, responding to his master's voice. "I love you too."

Robin lay against Scott before moving away reluctantly, knowing he had to cut the rope and the gloves sooner rather than later. He paused one last time to kiss his lover deeply, savoring every bit of him, wanting to draw this out for as long as possible. Scott was still in some faraway place, flying high from the intense scene.

Robin stepped away and reached into his bag to pull out the box cutter that he'd brought along when they heard the chime of the bell that announced an open door in the waiting room. Scott's eyes flew open, the panic and adrenaline shocking him back to reality, pushing Robin into action.

He cut the rope and slid the knife under each glove tearing the latex easily, and Scott hopped out of the chair, grabbing his clothes off the floor. Both men dressed quickly, pulling on jeans and throwing on their shirts, praying they'd be in time.

The door opened suddenly and Ron and Jenna stood there looking at them both in shock. "What the hell is going on here?" Ron asked, sweeping every corner of the room with a suspicious glance. He saw the bag in the corner, the red rope on the floor near the chair, the tube of K-Y Jelly sitting on the tray, and last but not least, the tied-off condom on the floor. It was almost comical watching his face as it reacted to everything, and the light bulb in his brain finally switched on, clueing him in to what he was seeing.

"You're fucking queers!" he accused in a voice filled with hatred.

"It's not what you think," Scott stammered, buttoning his shirt and brushing back his hair with a trembling hand.

"Don't tell me what I think! I know what I see."

"Maybe he had an emergency," Jenna chimed in, trying to diffuse the situation. "Did you guys see a patient?" she asked, giving Scott the opening he needed.

"Bullshit, Jenna! Look around you!" Ron spat out. His jowls were shaking with anger, making him look like an old bloodhound in full hunt.

"There's nothing to see!" Robin said forcefully. He too was trying to get himself together, straightening his T-shirt and pulling on his shoes one by one.

"I see two guys that have no business here smelling the way you do. This room reeks of sex!"

"Ron," Scott interjected, trying to appease him. "Let me explain."

"What's to explain? It's perfectly obvious, Scott. You're homos."

"Ron," Scott said again, trying to figure out what to say.

"Don't!" Ron spat out, putting his hand up in the universal signal for *stop*. He turned to Robin, twisting his lips in a malevolent sneer and said, "I should have known you were queer! No self-respecting male would be doing a woman's job!"

"Why, you piece of homophobic shit," Robin said. He swung and hit Ron square on the chin, more than satisfied when Ron's head snapped back and his eyes widened in pain.

"How does that feel coming from a nasty homo?" Robin asked.

"Get out of my office!" Ron said. "You're fired!"

"Too late," Robin yelled. "I quit the moment I hit you!"

"Please," Scott begged, getting in between the two and trying to make peace. "Ron, come on. You know Robin is great at what he does."

"I don't give a fuck if he's the best hygienist in the universe. I won't have any fruits in my office. And that goes for you too!"

"Ron? We're almost at the end of our contract. I've brought in a ton of money, and your practice is booming. Don't do this," Scott said in a voice filled with regret. "Don't get rid of me over some misguided thoughts about homosexuality."

"Misguided?" Ron looked at him in disbelief. "I'm not misguided. You are! Now get the fuck out of here."

"Are you sure you want to do this?" Scott asked.

"Scott! Don't you hear the man?" Robin butted in, grabbing hold of Scott's hand. "He wants us gone, so let's fucking go!"

Scott pulled his hand back quickly and said, "No! Why don't you go, Robin? Let me stay and talk to Ron."

"What?" Robin couldn't believe what he was hearing. He stared at Scott, disgusted with the whole turn of events but especially with the way Scott was behaving. He was enraged by Ron's power over his lover, turning him into a pathetic mess, denying who he was, pushing Robin away for a contract that was written in blood, as far as he was concerned. Their blood!

He spun around on his heels and walked out, leaving everything—the bag, the K-Y, the condom, but most importantly, his lover. He'd had enough.

Chapter 28

SCOTT stood in front of his desk, pulling drawers open and dumping everything into the box he'd brought from home. It was nine in the morning the day after the discovery. He'd spent the better part of yesterday afternoon and evening getting shit-faced, trying to mask the pain of his ruined life with shots of vodka, only ending up with a massive hangover and no solution. Robin had taken off, refusing to pick up any of his calls or respond to any text messages.

Scott couldn't blame him after the way he'd behaved and the things Ron had said. Robin was too proud and too sure of himself to put up with any more bullshit. He was probably already looking for another job, trying to get as far away from him and this office as possible.

The worst part of this was losing Robin. Scott had resigned himself to the loss of his job and his chance to step into this ready-made practice. That was made painfully obvious yesterday after he pleaded with Ron and begged him to reconsider, all to no avail. Ron was too caught up in his anger. He felt betrayed and humiliated by Scott and Robin, convinced that they'd taken advantage of him. He told Scott that he'd never work in San Francisco again, that he'd blackball him and denounce him at the next meeting of the San Francisco Dental Society and the American Academy of Periodontology.

Scott had tried to reason with him, to tell him that being gay had nothing to do with his ability as a dentist; however, Ron was having none of it. Even Jenna had surprised Scott with a show of support, trying to talk Ron into rethinking his decision and giving Scott another chance. He was taken aback by her gesture, unsure of where it was coming from, but grateful nonetheless.

Susie had walked in at eight in the morning, ready to start the day. She was completely unaware of what happened. Scott gave her a brief summary, and she offered to help with the packing, angered by Ron's attitude and disappointed that Scott was leaving. She was as devastated by Robin's departure as Scott, mourning the loss of a kind and loving friend because of a contemptuous man who had lost her respect months ago. She handed Scott a pile of books and watched him place it in the box, silently packing up the life he'd made for himself over the last nine months when the door burst open and Jenna stepped through looking completely agitated.

"Scott! You have to help us."

"What's wrong?" He couldn't imagine that they'd need his help for anything. He was told in no uncertain terms when he came in this morning that he was not to perform the implant surgery that was scheduled. Ron was going to do it despite Scott's protest. He felt sick to his stomach, knowing that his patient would be disappointed at seeing Ron instead of him. He'd built up a rapport with Bob Elliot over the last few months, finally gaining the millionaire's trust. Now, the trust was broken as he stepped away from the case in favor of Ron.

"He's perforated the sinus, and the implant is lost in the sinus cavity."

"What! How the fuck did you guys do that?"

"I don't know," Jenna said, suddenly losing all her composure. It was the first time Scott had ever seen this side of her. She was completely out of control, her eyes swam with tears and her voice was high-pitched and needy. "Scott, you have to help him."

"Give me one good reason why I should help the son-of-a-bitch! He brought this upon himself, and as far as I'm concerned, he can clean up his own mess."

She stepped forward and touched his arm, begging him. "Please—"

"No!" Scott said forcefully. "I'm not going to fix this. He can deal with Bob Elliot's wrath all by himself. I hope the man sues the pants off him."

"You owe him, Scott."

"What the fuck do you mean, Jenna? I owe him nothing!"

"You owe him your life, Scott. He's your father."

Scott looked at her in horror, backing away from her slowly. "No," he whispered, shaking his head in shock. He could feel his insides twisting in disgust, could actually feel the bile rushing up, the desire to vomit and cleanse himself paramount. He grabbed the glass of water that was handy and took a quick sip, pushing down the acid that was eating away at him. He turned to Susie, pleading silently, hoping for some guidance.

"What did you just say?" Susie asked Jenna, stepping forward quickly to stand beside Scott. She took his hand in hers and winced when he squeezed forcefully.

"You heard me," Jenna whispered in a voice heavy with sorrow.

"Does the mother fucker even know?" Susie asked, waiting for Jenna's reply.

"No, he doesn't," Jenna stated, finally breaking down and sobbing. The tears came in torrents streaking her face. She removed the safety glasses and mopped up her face with a tissue she'd grabbed off Scott's desk.

"You're lying, Jenna," Scott whispered, all the while looking at her in shock. "This is all a lie to make me help him. I won't do it!"

"I'm not, Scott! Do you think I wanted to tell you like this? I've spent thirty-three years keeping this secret. I would never have said anything if this hadn't happened."

"Bullshit!" Scott hurled, "Who are you anyway?"

"I'm your aunt! My sister, Anna, was your mother."

Scott fell into his chair, the anger knocked right out of him. "You knew my mother?" he looked up at Jenna, barely seeing her as his eyes filled with tears. "Why did she give me up?" he asked, craving the truth.

"She died, Scott. There were complications when you were born, and she died."

"No."

Jenna's tears continued to pour down her face, and Susie looked from her to Scott, finally realizing that their eyes were the exact same color, the leafy green that was Scott's signature, obviously a familial trait. She couldn't believe she'd missed this, but then again, it seemed like all of them had missed a lot of things in the last few months.

"Scott," Susie said, trying to pull this mess together. "Let's go in there and finish the surgery. No sense in Bob Elliot suffering because of Ron's incompetence. Come on. Wipe up your tears." She turned to Jenna and said, "We'll deal with you later. You have a lifetime of explaining to do."

"Yes," Jenna answered, calmed by their decision. "I'll tell you everything."

Scott moved in a trance, mindlessly doing what he was trained to do. He stepped over to the sink in the bathroom, rinsed off his face and washed his hands. When he emerged, he was Scott Gregory, competent surgeon. Gone was the needy man who'd just had the rug pulled out from underneath him. He and Susie made their way into the surgical suite to repair the damage Ron had inflicted on his patient.

Two hours later, the implant was retrieved and the perforated sinus bone grafted and repaired. Scott did a great job of undoing Ron's damage, never letting the patient know what had happened. Ron had stood there the entire time with Jenna, watching as Scott performed his magic with Susie assisting him. Ron only left the room when the last suture was sewn into place.

Scott left the patient in Susie's capable hands to administer the post-op instructions and answer whatever questions Bob Elliot might have. He made his way back to his office and quickly stripped off his scrubs and started putting on his street clothes when Ron came into the office and shut the door behind him.

"Thank you," Ron said begrudgingly.

"I didn't do it for you," Scott answered.

"I know, but I'm still grateful. You could have left me to flounder."

"I should have. You had no business performing that procedure."

"It's my practice! I can do whatever I want," Ron said, reverting back to his old indignant self.

"You are a menace," Scott said, getting into Ron's face. "A little bit of knowledge does not entitle you or give you the right to perform a procedure as delicate as a sinus lift. You could have seriously damaged Bob Elliot, and he would have won if he took you to court. Either quit doing this or find someone who knows what the fuck they're doing!"

"I've got you. Why look further?"

Scott stared at the man in front of him, desperate to feel some sort of connection. "You fired me, remember?"

"I can always change my mind," Ron said, smug in his belief that Scott would jump at this chance.

Scott looked into eyes that were nothing like his. In fact, there was nothing about Ron that would indicate that he was his biological parent. Scott was beginning to think that Jenna had lied to him just to save Ron's miserable ass.

"Let me out of here," Scott said, pushing Ron aside. "You make me sick!"

Ron grabbed at Scott, holding him back. "Look, I'm willing to forget what happened yesterday, so long as you promise me that you'll stop being a queer. I liked having you around."

"You mean you liked the money that I brought in."

"Sure. Who wouldn't?"

"Fuck you, Ron!" Scott pulled his arm out of Ron's grasp and pushed him away forcefully. "I may be a queer and in your eyes less than human, but I'm damn good at what I do. In fact, I'm fucking brilliant, and if you can't see that, if your opinion of me is influenced by the fact that I fuck men and not women, than you deserve to be alone, to end up a pauper, because no one in their right mind will want to partner with you once I get done telling them how incompetent you are!"

"I expect you back at your desk tomorrow."

"What about Robin?"

"Fuck that queer! I'll kill him if he so much as shows his fruity face around here."

"That fruit is my lover."

"Not if you want to stay in this practice. You'll have to give him up."

Scott grabbed the box off his desk and paused for a second. "What part of fuck off didn't you understand?"

The last thing he heard was Ron repeating himself, "Eight o'clock, Scott. Be here tomorrow."

ROBIN continued to ignore all of Scott's phone calls and messages. Scott ran a hand through his hair, practically tearing it out in frustration. He wanted to talk to Robin and tell him what had transpired since he walked out of the office yesterday. He needed advice, guidance from his friend and master, but all he was getting was the same recording over and over. "You know what to do, leave a message."

So he'd left several, each one needier than the last. He was sure that Robin had written him off as a lost cause. And he was probably right to do so. Scott was disgusted with himself; his need to belong overruling his common sense.

The doorbell rang, and he went to open it, stepping aside when Jenna walked through the door, followed by Susie, who had offered to pick her up and bring her to Scott's apartment.

"You want something to drink?" he asked both women.

"I'll have a beer, if you have it," Susie replied.

"Nothing for me," Jenna said, gnawing at her lip nervously. She'd never been to Scott's apartment, never actually sat down with him or Susie and had a normal conversation. All their contact had been at work, and it was usually all about Jenna telling them what to do.

Susie and Scott sat on one sofa and Jenna on the other. Finally, Susie broke the ice and said, "How old was your sister when she got knocked up?"

"She was barely seventeen," Jenna replied. "She and I were twins."

"You're kidding," Scott said. "Did she look like you?"

"Exactly like me, and that's what lead to all the problems."

"What do you mean?"

Jenna sighed and leaned her head back on the sofa. "I started working for Ron when I was a senior in high school. He was in his late twenties, had just graduated, and was recently married. He was handsome, Scott, and I was obsessed with him. I followed him around like a groupie; doing everything I could to attract his attention."

"What exactly did you do at the office? Did you assist him?"

"No. I was hired to help with the paperwork up at the front desk and do some light cleaning after hours. That's how it all started."

"So you came on to him, and he caved."

"Yeah."

"That piece of shit!" Susie said, disgusted. "He was a married man!"

"I was a slut," Jenna countered, "I basically seduced him."

"Oh, puh-leese," Susie said with an eye roll. "Don't make excuses for that mother fucker."

"It's true though. He didn't stand a chance. I was very pretty at seventeen," Jenna said, finally opening her eyes.

"How did your sister get into this?" Scott asked. "Please, don't tell me you guys had a three-way."

"No, nothing as exciting as that. I got sick with the flu, and Anna offered to work for me. We didn't say anything to Ron about her taking my place, and he just assumed she was me."

"So he fucked her, thinking she was you?" Scott stood, shocked beyond belief. He was not only a product of an illegitimate affair; his father hadn't even been fucking the right woman. "Jesus H. Christ!"

"I know it all sounds so stupid," Jenna said, "but Anna and I had a sibling rivalry that went beyond normal."

"You hated each other?" Scott was even more dismayed. He couldn't imagine having a blood relative and not loving them. Being an only child was one of his biggest regrets.

"Look, we loved each other deeply, the way that only twins can. We had a connection, but when I started sleeping with Ron, she got jealous and wanted to experience the same thing. I honestly think that she just wanted to sleep with him to see what it felt like to have sex. It wasn't an evil thing."

"And she got knocked up on her first try." Susie said, "That's messed up!"

"Why didn't she get an abortion?" Scott asked.

"We're Catholic," Jenna stated, as if that explained everything.

"I see," Scott replied with a shake of his head. "It's okay to sleep with a married man, but it's a mortal sin to get rid of the product of the affair."

"Something like that."

"Christ!"

"So what did you do?" Susie asked, caught up in the story.

"We'd been accepted at the University of North Carolina. She got pregnant that summer before we left for college, and when we got there, she hid it for a long time. Finally, she dropped out of school when it became too obvious. I was with her when she had the baby. She had you in a motel because we were too scared to go to the hospital."

"Sounds like a really bad soap opera," Susie said. "Did she die in the motel?"

"Yes. The bleeding never stopped, and I didn't know what to do," Jenna sat up and looked at them. She seemed tortured by the memory. "I couldn't help her," she whispered. "I did everything I could think of, but the blood just kept on coming."

"Jesus," Scott groaned. "What did you do when she finally died?"

"I called our parents. They were there in a few hours and took care of everything."

"Didn't they ask who the father was?"

"They were upset, Scott. They didn't press when I told them I didn't know. They just wanted to put you somewhere safe and forget everything."

"I was their first grandchild, wasn't I?"

"Yes, but you were born out of wedlock. You were only a source of shame for them."

"So they cleaned up the mess," Scott said, overwhelmed by Jenna's revelations. "What did they do with me?"

"They gave you up to the nuns," Jenna said, expecting him to understand. "Scott, it killed me; I really didn't want to them to do it, but I had no say, and I was protecting Anna's reputation."

"No, you weren't. You were protecting Ron."

Jenna was silent and finally she said, "You're right. I was still in love with him and didn't want him prosecuted."

"Jenna, he was married."

"I know, but I kept hoping he'd come to his senses."

"Well, he didn't, and you left your own flesh and blood for him."

"I left you in good hands," Jenna protested.

"You left me with strangers!" Scott's anger rushed through him, making him shake all over. He stood over Jenna and yelled, "You fucking gave me up like I was a piece of garbage!"

"No! It wasn't like that!" She started to cry again. Big droplets rolled down her cheeks, making her look younger than her fifty-three years. "We kept tabs on you, Scott. We found the Gregorys because we wanted to see you in a good home. My parents were not that heartless."

"Bullshit! You have no idea what I went through."

Jenna stood and moved over to Scott, trying to touch him but he backed away. "Get away from me!"

"How do you think you got here?" Jenna stated, wrestling control over her emotions. "Do you think this just happened? That he picked your name randomly?"

"Didn't he? Wasn't I chosen for my qualifications?" Scott was taken aback again, struck by yet another betrayal.

"I did it! I put your resume on top of the pile. I pushed for you, knowing that you should be here working for your father. You need to be with him, Scott. This is where you belong," Jenna said, her eyes a little wild with fear. "He needs you."

Scott froze, struck by Jenna's words. She was as crazy as Ron. So madly in love with a man who'd used her for years and taken her loyalty and love for granted, never acknowledging her needs.

"You're still in love with him, aren't you?" Scott asked.

"What does it matter? The important thing is that you need to be here with your father, working side by side with him," Jenna said, hoping to convince him, all the while moving toward Scott even as he kept backing away from her.

Susie was beside him suddenly, and he reached for her, grateful for her support. "I'm glad that I grew up somewhere else," Scott said as the realization hit him. "I'm sorry that my mother died and that I never got a chance to know her, but I'm not sorry that you left me. All these years, I've wondered what it would have been like to be with my real parents, and now I know that my life would have been hell."

"How do you figure? I care about you. And if Ron were to find out that you're his son, he'd give you everything."

"No, he wouldn't! He'd only help me if I were to give up who I am and what I believe. He'll never listen to my words or validate a single emotion if it doesn't coincide with his idea of 'normal'."

"What are you going to do with this information?" Jenna asked.

"Whatever I decide to do with it is my business. You have no say in my life."

"Scott. Let me tell him, he can make this all better."

"No! Jenna, you have some serious issues you need to deal with, as do I. Ron Morris is not the solution to my problems."

"But he is, Scott. Can't you see that?"

"No, I don't see it your way. Now please leave my house. I'll be glad to pay for a taxi, just get the fuck out of here. I can't stand the sight of you."

Chapter 29

SCOTT made his way out of San Francisco and headed for the East Bay. He was determined to put the city and all its revelations behind him, at least for the time being. The ride out to San Ramon was no longer than usual, but it seemed interminable to him. He yearned for Robin's presence, needed to feel his arms around him, and craved his support and his love.

What happened today had been life-altering. It had opened his eyes to many things, the most important one being his love and respect for a man who'd accepted him at face value, despite his insecurities, his kinks, and his hang-ups over his lack of family or roots. Robin had loved him unconditionally, which seemed huge right now, considering the recent discovery that he'd been abandoned like yesterday's trash.

The worst part was the fact that he had Ron Morris's genes running through his body. That thought alone was freaking him out more than anything else. He was convinced that Robin wouldn't want to have anything to do with him since he was the bastard of a homophobic prick. He hoped that he was wrong and Robin would tell him that it didn't matter. But the insecure side of him was winning the argument in his head, convincing him that Robin would turn away.

He got to the complex where Denise Kennedy lived, and he parked the car and made his way up to the small apartment. It wasn't much to look at, but every time he and Robin had come here they'd been happy. He rang the doorbell and was surprised when Denise opened the door, not Robin.

"Scott? What brings you here?"

"I'm looking for Robin."

"Isn't he with you?"

"No," Scott said slowly. The fact that Robin hadn't come home to Denise said a lot about his state of mind. He was MIA, and Scott felt the fear climbing up his spine like a nasty insect. "Where do you think he might be?"

"I haven't the foggiest," Denise said, starting to worry as well. "Did you guys have a fight?"

"Sort of, well, not really, but I guess you could call it that," Scott stuttered and stopped, embarrassed to be answering to his lover's mother.

"Scott, sweetie, that's as clear as mud. Speak English and enunciate. Did you or didn't you have a fight?"

"We did."

"You need to talk to someone, and I'm here. Now, come in and tell me all about it." She pulled him in, not waiting for him to say yes or no.

"Are you hungry or thirsty?"

"No."

"Okay." Denise sat at the small kitchen table with him. "What happened?"

"I don't think I can tell you, it's really personal."

"Honey, you don't have to give me details. I'm pretty familiar with Robin and his world, so there's not much you can tell me that will shock me."

Scott had no idea if Denise knew about their D/s relationship. He couldn't imagine a mother talking to her child about any of that, but he'd heard her and Robin kidding around, and he knew that she was comfortable with the love they had for each other. He decided to approach the conversation from that angle and leave out the domination part of their partnership.

"We got caught by our boss, my so-called partner."

"No! Where did he catch you?"

"At the office."

"You were having sex at work?" Denise was a little taken aback, not about the sex, but about having it at the office. "That was kind of dumb, wasn't it?"

"It was."

"Okay, moving right along," she said, sitting up straighter. "What happened next?"

"Ron sort of lost it, and Robin got upset and hit him."

"He didn't!"

"Ron insulted him, Denise! He told him that he wasn't surprised he was a queer since he was doing a woman's job."

"Why that fucking son of a bitch!" Denise said, bristling for a fight. "Did Robin get him good?"

"Oh, yeah, he got him good, and then he quit!"

"That's my boy," Denise smiled. "He's a pistol."

Scott smiled back. "He sure is."

"So why did he take off?"

"I was trying to make peace with Ron, and I sort of pushed Robin away and asked him to go."

"I see. *Did* you choose Ron over Robin?"

"I was confused, Denise," Scott rationalized, "I thought I was doing the right thing, but I realize now that it was a mistake. I've been trying to tell him I was wrong, but he refuses to answer any of my calls. Where do you think he is?"

"Wish I knew, sweetie. He'll turn up eventually. He always does."

"There's something else, Denise. Something I found out since Robin left the city. It's bad."

"What could be worse than losing your job?"

"Did you know I was adopted?"

"No."

"Well, I was. I knew nothing about my heritage, where I came from, or anything about my biological parents, and it's been an issue of mine."

"That's understandable, sweetie," Denise said gently, reaching across the table to take his hand in hers. "Are you close to your adoptive parents?"

"They're good people, but we never really connected," Scott admitted. "It's probably my fault, because I never really gave them the opportunity to be real parents. I was always looking for my past, for the perfect family that only existed in my head, and they kept coming up short."

"Eventually you're going to have to let this go, Scott."

"Well, here's the kicker, Denise. I found out yesterday who my real parents are, and you know that saying 'be careful what you wish for'?"

"Yeah."

"Well, I wish that I had never found out."

"Why?"

"My father, my real biological father, is Ron Morris, the biggest piece of shit in this world."

"Oh my," Denise said, giving Scott's hand a tight squeeze. "I'm so sorry, sweetie. What about your mother? Did you find out about her?"

"It's a bizarre story."

"Tell me," she said, knowing he needed to let it all out.

He started to talk and talk, giving her all the background and details, telling her about his shock and anger at Jenna and Ron. Finally he looked at Denise. "He's going to hate me now, isn't he?"

"Why would he possibly hate you? He loves you, Scott. Passionately."

"How could he possibly love me? Look where I come from?"

"Oh sweetie," Denise stood up and went over to Scott. "Get up and give me a hug," she said, wrapping her arms around her son's beautiful but vulnerable man. "You are a very lovable individual, and my son has decided that you're the one he wants to spend the rest of his life with. He's not going to give you up because your parents are not perfect."

"How could he possibly love me after all that?"

"After what? You had nothing to do with this. You're exactly like Robin, a victim of a drive-by fucking."

"What?" He looked at her like she'd lost her mind. "What did you just say?"

"Come over here and let me tell you something I've never told anyone, including Robin," Denise moved them over to the sofa, and she sat down and got comfortable. "I was raped when I was in my late twenties. It happened one night while I was walking home from work. I was assaulted and raped, left for dead. But guess what? I didn't die. I got knocked up!"

"Robin?"

"Yes, Robin. He's the most wonderful person in my world. The kindest, most sensitive, caring man I know, and his father is a criminal. So don't tell me that Robin will never want you because of your parents. Don't ever use that line in my presence, because it won't fly," Denise said fiercely. "I believe in nurture, not nature. I don't care who your biological parents are, Scott. Your adoptive parents did a fine job with you, from what I can see."

"They did, and I never realized it until now."

"Well, pick up the fucking phone and tell them once in a while. I'm sure they'd like to hear it."

Scott smiled at Denise tenderly. "You're quite amazing, you know that?"

"No, I'm not, sweetie. Now give me a big hug and let's try and figure out where Robin is."

ROBIN was at the BDSM club in San Ramon, trying to forget what had happened. He'd come to drown his sorrows and had ended up staying and working a few shifts at the bar, eventually falling into bed in one of the rooms in back. It was mindless work, something he could do automatically, and it helped to keep him from going back to the city and beating Ron Morris to a pulp.

He knew he should have gone home to Denise, but he didn't want to worry her, nor did he want her to feel that she had to support him or ask him to move back to her apartment. He had enough money put away to sustain him for a few months until he found another job, but right now, the last thing he wanted to do was go on interviews. He needed time to mourn his loss, to forget Scott and all they'd shared. This whole business of being in love sucked big time.

He was still hurting from Scott's rejection. It was worse than any physical blow, especially after everything they'd experienced. He knew that what happened was partially his fault. He should have used better judgment, but Scott was just as much to blame. It killed him to walk away, but Scott had obviously made his choice—it was money and career over him. Case closed.

So he went on a bender, getting piss-eyed drunk, flirting with anything that moved, and ending up in bed by himself. The thought of kissing anyone other than Scott was repugnant, but he knew that he had to get over it, move on with his life, and what better way than to have sex with someone else, to lose himself in a scene with another sub? He was done wishing for the happy ending. Scott had made his choice, and he wasn't a part of it.

His shift had ended, and he made his way through the crowd, scanning faces to see if he found anyone remotely interesting. He knew it would be a push to get into someone else this soon, but he had to do it. He settled on a familiar face. Joe had been one of his regulars, a nice guy, into knife play. It would take his mind off Scott for at least an hour or so. He was moving toward Joe when he was stopped by a hand that reached out to him and pulled him back roughly.

"Where the hell do you think you're going?" Scott asked, jealous. He'd seen that predatory look in Robin before, and he'd be damned if he was going to let someone else hone in on his gig.

"What the fuck do you care?" Robin asked, startled by Scott's presence. "Why are you here, anyway?"

"I've come to take you back home," Scott replied, confident, possessive.

Robin laughed. "Home? I am home!"

"No, you're not."

"Listen, Scott, this is where I belong, with men just like me. We're secure in our world, fucked up as it might be for anyone else looking in. We're gay, and we're into the scene and not ashamed of it."

"Ouch," Scott replied. "I suppose I deserved that."

"Damn right! I'm done playing games, fucking around with Ron Morris. You've made your choice," Robin said in no uncertain terms despite the fact that his eyes were swimming with tears.

"Would you change your mind if I told you that I walked away from Ron? That I'm sorry, that I love you more than any fucking contract or anyone else in the world?"

"Do you?" Robin asked, looking at Scott intently. His eyes were just as green as they were in his recurring fantasies, his lips just as enticing. He was the most beautiful man Robin ever laid his eyes on, bar none, and he was here, humbling himself, begging for forgiveness.

"Robin, I choose you. I'm done pretending. I want you back in my life as my partner, my master, my lover, and my friend. Please, come back with me?" Scott didn't care that his tears were falling and people were watching them, enjoying the drama.

"Baby," Robin whispered, wiping away a tear with his thumb. "Don't look at me like that. You know I can never resist a man begging."

Scott choked on a laugh and moved into Robin's embrace, pressing his face against Robin's neck. He inhaled, taking in a deep, ragged breath, losing himself in Robin's smell, in the feel of the hard body holding him tightly, in the arms that wrapped around him, strong and dominant, sure of himself and his position in Scott's life.

"Tell me what you want, love?" Robin had lifted Scott's face and was staring at him with eyes that were dusky with need. "Say it, baby."

"Show me how much you love me, Red."

"My way?"

Robin's breath was warm and sweet; he licked Scott's lips, sucked on them for a second, drawing out the moan that came with the gentle bite, and he pulled back for a second to hear the answer.

"Yes," Scott whispered. "The only way."

MICKIE B. ASHLING is the penname for a responsible office manager by day and a writer of steaming M/M erotica by night. Mickie loves men, starting with her four grown sons, her dog Charlie, and her male cat, Calvin. She's surrounded by them at every turn, and she continues this romance with everything male by writing love stories about men who love men. Nothing can ignite her muse faster than the thought of two hunky guys getting it on. Her family despairs of this need but has quietly given up on her. She's promised them that someday she'll write a het romance, but no one who really knows her is holding their breath.

Visit Mickie's blogs at http://mickieashling.livejournal.com and http://www.mickiebashling.blogspot.com.

For more of the
best M/M romance,
visit

Dreamspinner Press

www.dreamspinnerpress.com